TRUMPED
AN ALTERNATIVE MUSICAL

This edition first published in 2020 by Blue Lens
Blue Lens is an imprint of Blue Lens Films Limited

Blue Lens Films Limited, 71-75 Shelton Street,
Covent Garden, London, WC2H 9JQ, United Kingdom

ISBN 978 1 913408 56 5
1 3 5 9 10 8 6 4 2

Printer and binder may vary between territories of
production and sale

LICENSE INFORMATION

Subject to the terms and conditions set out in this book,
the purchase* of this book entitles you to be granted a
one-time non-transferable performance license for the
material with the following conditions:

VERSION	TRUMPED: An Alternative Musical, Part Two (Act III & IV)
LICENSE TYPE	Amateur Two Performance *See terms for eligibility criteria*
LICENSE AREA	Australia, Canada, European Economic Area, New Zealand, South Africa, United Kingdom, United States
NUMBER OF PERFORMANCES	Maximum of two performances
MAXIMUM AUDIENCE	Not to exceed 250 in aggregate
TICKET PRICE RESTRICTIONS	Not to exceed USD 8.00 (or foreign equivalent) per ticket, or USD 1,200 (or foreign equivalent) in aggregate.

*Only the first purchaser of this book is entitled to be
granted a performance license. Used or resold copies do not
entitle you to a performance license.

To register for your license, please complete the online
for at analternativemusical.com/performancelicenses.

TERMS OF LICENSE

1) Subject to these terms, the first purchaser of this book ("the licensee") (defined as the individual/ organization to first purchase this copy from a recognized registered book retailer), is entitled to be granted by Toupee or Not Toupee Limited (a UK based company managing the rights to TRUMPED: An Alternative Musical on behalf of the rights holders), a one-time non-transferable performance or use license for the material contained within this book.
2) No performance license will be granted for purchasers of used or resold copies of this book.
3) No performance or performance-related work may begin until a performance license has been granted to the licensee.
4) The granting of a performance license is subject to the successful registration of the licensee and their purchase of this book. Satisfactory proof of first purchase is required before a license is granted.
5) Licensees can register their book purchase at analternativemusical.com/performancelicenses.
6) The license must register before January 1, 2022. No license will be granted for registrations after this date. All licenses (except educational use) will be valid for a period of twelve months. Any and all performance-related work and performances must take place within this period. Educational use licenses will be valid for a period of three months. Any use, performance-related work or performances undertaken outside of this period will be deemed unlicensed use.
7) Licenses will be granted subject to the terms and with the conditions as set out within this book. License terms or conditions will not be varied under any circumstance.
8) Only one license will be granted per book and each licensee is limited to a maximum of five licenses.
9) Educational licenses are available only to registered non-profit educational organizations within the license area.
10) Non-profit licenses are available only to registered non-profit organizations within the license area.
11) Amateur licensees are available only to amateur performance groups within the license area and with annual revenues not exceeding USD 25,000 (or foreign equivalent) in the previous financial year.

12) Licenses are valid only within the license area, defined as: The United States, United Kingdom, European Economic Area, Canada, Australia, New Zealand, and South Africa.

13) Once a purchase is registered, a license cannot be canceled for any reason.

14) Once a license is granted, the licensee is required to enter the license number on each page of this book in the designated area, after which, copies of the material may be made in order to distribute for performance or education use as the license allows. No copying is permitted without a license number being entered on each page. Licensees are required to control and note the number of copies of the material being made. All copies must be returned to the licensee and destroyed at the end of the material's licensed use.

15) Once licensed, subject to the conditions of that license and these terms, the licensee is permitted to produce the material contained within this book for public performance. This does not apply to educational use licenses which grant the license to use the material in a purely educational environment with performances permitted to non-paying audiences not exceeding 30 persons.

16) Licensees must produce the material in full with no edits of any kind (substitutions, additions or subtractions) permitted. In the circumstance of extract licenses, the licensee is permitted to choose up to fifteen scenes to produced. These scenes must be produced in full with no edits of any kind (substitutions, additions or subtractions) permitted.

17) Performances must take place at a premises which is owned and/or controlled by the licensee. No performances may take place as part of a festival in any territory or within 50 miles of a city where a current arts festival is taking place during that festival.

18) No additional rights, including, but not limited to, artwork, likeness, trademarks (registered or otherwise), or any other intellectual property is included as part of any license. No license is granted for any music, tune, incidental music, or any other material which may, in some circumstances, be held by third party rights holders.

19) Licensees are required to observe all relevant local, state, and national laws, and any relevant union agreement. Under no circumstances will the retailer, distributor, publisher, Toupee or Not Toupee Limited, the

rights holders, or any other third party be liable to the licensee or any person, group, or organization associated with the licensee, for any loss or liability which the licensee experiences or which is incurred as a result of a license being granted.

20) In no circumstance will the livability of the retailer, distributor, publisher, Toupee or Not Toupee Limited, the rights holders, or any other third party be liable to the licensee or any person, group, or organization associated with the licensee, exceed the United States list price of this book at the time of purchase.

21) For performances taking place in the United Kingdom or the European Economic Area, the licensee may be required to pay VAT in addition to the purchase of this book. No performance license will be granted until this is paid.

22) The licensee and any person, group, or organization associated with the licensee, must not bring the the retailer, distributor, publisher, Toupee or Not Toupee Limited, the rights holders, or any other third party into disrepute. This includes, but is not limited to, by sharing hateful messages and/or content, and using the licensed material in any way except that explicitly permitted in their license. Should Toupee or Not Toupee Limited decide that the licensee or any person, group, or organization associated with the licensee has breached this term, the license granted will be revoked without compensation to the licensee.

23) The licensee must ensure that they do not associate themselves or lead any person to believe they are associated with the retailer, distributor, publisher, Toupee or Not Toupee Limited, the rights holders, or any other third party.

24) Should the purchaser of this book be ineligible for a license, no refund of this book will be given. Should the licensee breach any term or condition of the license, the license granted will be revoked without compensation to the licensee.

INTRODUCTION

Written in four acts presented across two parts, TRUMPED:
An Alternative Musical is a satirical stage play that
parodies the 2016 Presidential Election campaign of Donald
Trump and his subsequent time in office as the 45th
President of the United States.

Opening on the final day of the July 2016 Republican
National Convention in Cleveland, Ohio, Act I tells the
story behind the Trump campaign's journey from the outsider
of the Republican field to the unexpected winner of the
Electoral College with a questionable victory.

Covering the Russia meeting at Trump Tower, all three
election debates against the Democratic opponent, Hillary
Clinton, and the attempts of the Russian President,
Vladimir Putin, to ensure a win for the Trump campaign in
the state of Wisconsin, Act I concludes at the end of
November 8, election day, as the final results come in.

With the election over and Donald Trump set to become the
4th President, Act II opens the day following the election
as both the world and the current President, Barack Obama,
are all still in shock at the previous day's result.

Concluding toward the end of Trump's first year in office,
Act II covers his and his Vice President, Mike Pence's
inaugurations, a visit to the White House by his German
counterpart, Angela Merkel, and the apparent early collapse
of the Trump regime brought about through the actions of
Robert Mueller, the tweets of Donald Trump Junior, and the
gullibility of Eric Trump, forcing the family to make a
quick escape and leave another to fall in their place as
Part One comes to a close.

Picking up some weeks after the conclusion of Part One, Act
III opens as the President is presumed missing by his
closet supporters, and Vladimir Putin is becoming tiresome
of ruling from the front lines.

With the job of bringing Trump back to the United States
tasked to him, Fox News anchor, Sean Hannity, soon sets off
to South America to discover that his journey home is to

(CONTINUED)

CONTINUED:

be hindered by the measures he supported.

Coming to a close as the 2018 Midterm elections approach, Act III follows the President as, despite his America-first attitude, he attempts to forge new international ties with world leaders and royalty alike, while domestically, his party works to secure a new seat on the Supreme Court.

Act IV opens with an opportunity to discover how Trump's predecessor is coping with his post-presidential life and his thoughts on the upcoming Midterm elections. Leaving island life behind, the action then returns to Trump as he discovers that under his leadership, the Republican Party is set for a historic loss.

Following the Midterms being brought to you live from Florida and Texas, Act IV goes on to tell the story of a government shutdown and fine dining Trump-style as the Democrats begin searching for their 2020 nominee.

Coming to a close in late 2019, this final act builds up to an interpretation of events as they should have been, with the President finally being held to account.

CAST OF CHARACTERS

All characters are listed in order of appearance.

HILLARY CLINTON, Presidential Candidate/ Former Sec. State
FOX NEWS PRODUCER, Producer for Fox & Friends
STEVE DOOCY, Fox & Friends Host
AINSLEY EARHARDT, Fox & Friends Host
BRIAN KILMEADE, Fox & Friends Host
THE NARRATOR, Narrator of TRUMPED: An Alternative Musical
VLADIMIR PUTIN, President of Russia/ American Supreme Ruler
SEAN HANNITY, Fox News Anchor
IVANKA TRUMP, Daughter to Donald Trump
ERIC TRUMP, Son to Donald Trump/ Eric
DONALD TRUMP, Presidential Candidate/ 45th President
DONALD TRUMP JR, Son to Donald Trump
DMITRY SUREFIRE, Agent of the Kremlin
PETROV SUREFIRE, Agent of the Kremlin
MICHAEL COHEN, Lawyer to Donald Trump
JARED KUSHNER, Son-in-Law and Advisor to Donald Trump
MIKE PENCE, Running Mate to Donald Trump/ Vice-President
KELLYANNE CONWAY, Campaign Manager to Donald Trump
JUSTICE KENNEDY, Supreme Court Justice
ANGELA MERKEL, Chancellor of Germany
EMMANUEL MACRON, President of France
JUSTIN TRUDEAU, Prime Minister of Canada
PRINCE PHILIP, Husband to The Queen
PRINCE CHARLES, Son to The Queen
THE QUEEN, The Queen of the United Kingdom
GUARD, Buckingham Place Guard
PRESS #1, CNN Journalist
PRESS #3, Washington Post Journalist
PRESS #4, NBC Journalist
PRESS #5, Fox News Journalist
PRESS #6, MSNBC Journalist
JUDGE, Member of the Judiciary
BARTENDER, Bartender in DC
BRETT KAVANAUGH, Supreme Court Justice Nominee
JOHN CORNYN, Senator from Texas
TED CRUZ, Senator from Texas
JEFF FLAKE, Senator from Arizona
LINDSEY GRAHAM, Senator from South Carolina
CHUCK GRASSLEY, Senator from Iowa
ORRIN HATCH, Senator from Utah

(CONTINUED)

CONTINUED:

DIANNE FEINSTEIN, Senator from California
SUSAN COLLINS, Senator from Maine
ANDERSON COOPER, CNN News Anchor/ Second Debate Moderator
BARACK OBAMA, 44th President
WAITER, Tahiti Restaurant Waiter
MITCH MCCONNELL, Senate Majority Leader from Kentucky
PRESS #2, New York Times Journalist
NANCY PELOSI, Speaker of the House
CHUCK SCHUMER, Senate Minority Leader from New York
LOCAL, Texas Local
STORE OWNER, Texas Store Owner
BETO O'ROURKE, Democratic Senate and Presidential Candidate
ELECTION OFFICIAL, Election Official
LESTER HOLT, NBC News Anchor/ First Debate Moderator
MARTHA RADDATZ, ABC News Anchor/ Second Debate Moderator
MARCO RUBIO, Senator from Florida
MOTHER, Texas Mother
JIM ACOSTA, CNN White House Correspondent
SARAH HUCKABEE SANDERS, White House Press Secretary
INTERN, White House Intern
PAUL RYAN, Speaker of the House
ELIZABETH WARREN, Senator from Massachusetts/ 49th VP
JOE BIDEN, Former Vice President/ 46th President
BERNIE SANDERS, Senator from Vermont/ Democratic Candidate
GENERIC WHITE MAN, Democratic Presidential Candidate
GEORGE CONWAY, Husband to Kellyanne Conway
RACHEL MADDOW, MSNBC News Anchor/ Dem. Debate Moderator
CHUCK TODD, MSNBC News Anchor/ Dem. Debate Moderator
KAMALA HARRIS, Senator from California/ Dem. Candidate
PETE BUTTIGIEG, Mayor of South Bend/ Dem. Candidate
MARIANNE WILLIAMSON, Dem. Candidate
ADAM SCHIFF, House Intelligence Committee Chair
DEVIN NUNES, Congressman from California/ Farmer
ERIC SWALWELL, Congressman from California
ROBERT MUELLER, Former FBI Director/ Special Counsel
JIM JORDAN, Congressman from Ohio
MATT GAETZ, Congressman from Florida
SMALL BOY, Donald Trump Fan
CASHIER, Store Cashier
TIFFANY TRUMP, Daughter to Donald Trump
FBI AGENT #1, Agent for the FBI
FBI AGENT #2, Agent for the FBI

PRODUCTION NOTES

At all performances, the production crew should ensure that a message is played to audiences in order to inform them that while based upon and satirizing true events, TRUMPED: An Alternative Musical, Part One and Two, should not be considered a true or accurate record or representation of those events, nor should it be considered to portray the individuals satirized within accurately.

At all performances, a seat should be resaved at the end of the row within the audience for the character of Hillary Clinton to make her entrance from in Act I, Scene 7. This seat should be within the front orchestra section and be viewable, as far as reasonably possible, by all sections of the auditorium.

To cover the high number of characters within TRUMPED: An Alternative Musical, the majority of company members should perform multiple roles. This excludes the company member who is playing the role of the Narrator.

Where the script refers to the Ensemble, this should be taken to mean all company members, who are available at the time of that scene (i.e., not performing a different role within the scene or undertaking a wardrobe change), except for where specific exemptions are noted within the script.

The note that follows the introduction of the ensemble provides additional information on the role which the ensemble is performing in that scene (e.g., "ENSEMBLE (as PRESS").

In some instances, specific characters will be included as part of the ensemble (e.g., "Press #1").

At no point should company members performing the role of the Narrator or Donald Trump be included within the ensemble.

Performances of TRUMPED: An Alternative Musical should not require additional ensemble members outside of principal company members and understudies.

(CONTINUED)

CONTINUED:

The role of the Narrator is nonspecific for casting purposes, and freedom should be offered to this company member to perform their own style of narration (within the direction of the written material and director).

With the majority of characters in TRUMPED: An Alternative Musical based upon real people and to be performed as impersonations and parodies, company members should be given the freedom (within the direction of the written material and director) to perform the impersonation as they feel most appropriate. This may include the changing of minor words, the mispronunciation of words and phrases, or varying the pace of delivery.

"Cardboard Melania" should be achieved through the creation of a life-size cardboard cutout of Melania Trump being attached to an RC vehicle, which is controlled from offstage.

<u>Dialogue</u>	Indicates that dialogue should be mispronounced.
Dialogue	Indicates that dialogue should be emphasized.
/DIALOGUE/	Indicates that dialogue should be sung.

PART TWO

ACT III : "THE SECOND YEAR"

ACT III, PRE-SHOW | PRE-SHOW

>   As the audience returns to the
>   auditorium for phase two, they
>   are greeted by a stage which is
>   lit by a sidle center spotlight.
>
>   In the middle of the spotlight,
>   a gravestone stands atop a small
>   mound of earth with the words
>   "R.I.P. America," etched into
>   the stone.
>
>   Once the audience is seated, the
>   lights in the auditorium go
>   down, and the voice of HILLARY
>   CLINTON fills the room.

                    CLINTON (PRE-RECORDED)
Hello again, America. It is Hillary Rodham Clinton here
once more. Still here. Oh, I am still here. Of course, I am
still here. I am not going anywhere. I never have, and I
never will. You do not get rid of Hillary Rodham Clinton
that easily.

I am here to welcome all of you, whether you be a man, a
woman, a small man, or even a small woman - unless you did
not vote for me, that is. If that is the case, then I think
that I speak for all of us when I say that you can go off
and have some sexual intercourse with yourself. To the rest
of you, welcome to this here performance of part two of
TRUMPED: An Alternative Musical. Still one-hundred percent
James Corden free.

This second part of the show is the sequel to the first
part of the show. The only sequel. Please, let this be the
only sequel. Please, god. We are all really going to need
to face some facts here, America. There may be some very
difficult choices ahead.
                         (MORE)
                                              (CONTINUED)

CONTINUED:

                              CLINTON (PRE-RECORDED) (CONT'D)
And I am not talking about whether it is time to put
Florida out of its misery. I am talking about the wall.
If some of us are stupid enough actually to vote for that
man a second time, then we really are going to need it. We
are going to need it so that we all have something to bash
our heads against daily in frustration.

Before this performance gets underway, I would just like to
remind you once again that you need to switch off all of
your mobile phones and other electronic devices. If Mike
Pence sees any of them, then he might attempt to set up
witch trials again, and the last time he did that, I lost
my first primary.

Also, Russia. Russia might be using them to listen in, and
the producers of this show would rather they did not know
what was is in. They have not yet trained to run away fast
enough.

So sit back and relax... Well, not back and probably not
relax. Trump is still the President after all, and none of
us have been able to do either for some time. Instead, sit
forward and tense, or in the fetal position crying in the
nearest corner with a gentle, comforting rocking motion.

Finally, thank you for your co-operation and remember to
vote for me the next time I run for office. I will even
offer you Bernie's policy of healthcare for all, because
let us face it, by the time that I am finally president, we
are all going to be of an age where it would come in really
useful.

Please enjoy the show.

                         The spotlight fades, and the
                         stage falls into darkness.

ACT III, SCENE ONE | FOX & FRIENDS

                         For a short moment, the stage
                         remains dark.

                                                    (CONTINUED)

                    FOX NEWS PRODUCER (OFF)
Please get into position. We're ready to go live.

                              Lights up on the FOX & FRIENDS
                              STUDIO in New York City.

                              Sat on a couch ready to present
                              their show live to the nation,
                              STEVE DOOCY, AINSLEY EARHARDT,
                              and BRIAN KILMEADE. EARHARDT is
                              busy tidying KILMEADE's suit as
                              the FOX NEWS PRODUCER enters.

                              Opening title music begins to
                              play.

                    FOX NEWS PRODUCER
And we are live in five... four... three... two... and
go...

                              The FOX NEWS PRODUCER exits.

                    DOOCY
Good morning, patriots.

                    EARHARDT
You know, Steve? I heard that it's a good morning too.
Hello there, America.

                    DOOCY
It's not just a good morning, though, is it, Ainsley?

                    EARHARDT
That's right, Steve. It's also a very good start to the
week, isn't it?

                    DOOCY
That's right, Ainsley. Happy Monday, loyal subjects.

                    EARHARDT
How was your weekend, Brian?

                    KILMEADE
It was exciting.

                                        (CONTINUED)

                    EARHARDT
That's great --

                    KILMEADE
I got to fly in a helicopter when it came to rescue me from
a lake after I fell in the water while fishing. I couldn't
swim back to my boat because I was scared by what I thought
was a shark in the water. But it wasn't a shark, it was
just my reflection.

                    EARHARDT
Great.

                    KILMEADE
I think it was a hammerhead, actually.

                    DOOCY
Well, do you know what is not so great today, Ainsley?

                    EARHARDT
I don't, Steve. Why don't you tell me and all of those who
are watching us at home?

                    DOOCY
I'll do just that, Ainsley. It's not great that nobody
knows where the President is right now. He hasn't been seen
for weeks.

                    EARHARDT
That's right, Steve. If you're watching us today, Mister
Trump, let us know that you're okay. Send us a sign.

                    KILMEADE
I think our viewers are very rude. We are always telling
them things, but they never tell us anything back.

                    EARHARDT
What do you think has happened to the President, Brian?

                    KILMEADE
Perhaps he's not very well?

                    DOOCY and EARHARDT both laugh.

                                            (CONTINUED)

DOOCY
Ha. Ha. Ha. That's very funny, Brian.

EARHARDT
But what an absurd suggestion. Our President could never be
ill. He's far too healthy for that.

DOOCY
That's right, Ainsley. Remember, Brian, his last medical
showed us that he's a healthy two hundred and thirty-nine
pounds.

KILMEADE
Does anyone know what that is in Dollars?

EARHARDT
Perhaps he's been kidnapped?

KILMEADE
By Hillary Clinton?

EARHARDT
You know, that could be true, Brian.

DOOCY
It wouldn't surprise me.

EARHARDT
Not at all, Steve.

DOOCY
Well, that really is some breaking news happening on Fox
and Friends this morning. Our President has been kidnapped
by none other than Hillary Clinton. You heard it here
first.

EARHARDT
Perhaps she is hiding him in the same place that she has
been hiding all of those emails from the American people,
Steve?

                    CLINTON enters.

                                              (CONTINUED)

                          CLINTON
Seriously? I mean, seriously? Why are you people all still
so obsessed with me? The election was over a year ago.

                          DOOCY
Was it really over a year ago, though? Or is the concept of
time just a liberal conspiracy against real Americans.

                          CLINTON
You know what? Just delete your program.

                    KILMEADE begins to cheer.

                          EARHARDT
She isn't being nice to us, Brian. The nasty woman said a
bad thing.

                          KILMEADE
Oh.

                    KILMEADE stops cheering and
                    instead begins to cry.

                          KILMEADE
That was the meanest thing anyone has ever said to me.

                          EARHARDT
It's okay, Brian. Isn't it, Steve?

                          DOOCY
That's right, Ainsley.
                         (to CLINTON)
Look at what you've done now. You've made Brian cry.

                          KILMEADE
I want my mom.

ACT III, SCENE TWO | PUTIN IN THE OVAL OFFICE

                         The NARRATOR enters at the front
                         of an otherwise dark stage.

                                          (CONTINUED)

                         NARRATOR
And so we return when some weeks have passed since Donald
J. Trump handed over his mast to another which prompted
within the White House a notable change of cast.

It was Jared Kushner who took the fall, and off to jail he
was ordered when on Trump he refused to talk or even
scrawl. But still seeks Mueller for answers and truth,
though with the dynasty out of the way, it is much harder
to sleuth.

Meanwhile, across America, opinions are mixed, with some to
say the President's departure was one to save the nation
from certain doom. In contrast, others feel he did little
to help when he boarded that flight to South America while
upon his foot, paper from an airport bathroom.

Though one fact cannot be disputed --

                                   The NARRATOR is interrupted by
                                   the entrance of a cloaked figure
                                   of "death."

                                   As the figure approaches, it
                                   removes its hood to reveal that
                                   they are actually CLINTON
                                   dressed in a black Grim Reaper
                                   pantsuit.

                         NARRATOR
Hillary, what are you doing here?

                         CLINTON
Me? Oh, well, I'm just here to remind all of these fine
American people in the audience that I do still exist.

                                   CLINTON begins to wave at the
                                   audience.

                         NARRATOR
But weren't you here doing that just a moment ago

                                                        (CONTINUED)

                    CLINTON
Well, yes, I was. But in these current times, things happen
quickly, and people forget easily.

                              CLINTON points at an audience
                              member in the front row.

                    CLINTON
                 (to audience member)
It's you. Hello! How good to see you again... for the very
first time. How are you?

                    NARRATOR
Why are you dressed like that?

                    CLINTON
Like this? It is a costume. I have decided that it would be
appropriate for me to embrace my pure form and become the
ghost of elections past.

                    NARRATOR
But you don't look like a ghost. You're closer to a grim
reaper.

                    CLINTON
I know that. But I was talking to Bill, and he reckons that
the whole point of dressing up is to look different from
how you usually do.

                    NARRATOR
I still don't understand why you're dressing up.

                    CLINTON
I want to be able to take my rightful place in the Oval
Office, and so I am here to watch over the slow and painful
death of Donald Trump's political career.

                    NARRATOR
In the same way he did to you?

                    CLINTON
No. In fact, he did not do that. Something cannot die if it
is already dead. And you can trust me on that.
                    (MORE)

                                                (CONTINUED)

CONTINUED:
                         CLINTON (CONT'D)
I searched it up on the internet. Or as the cool people
say, I went and **Binged** it.

                         NARRATOR
Google?

                         CLINTON
No. Google is what Bill and I save for our special
quadrennial date nights. Or as most people call them, the
midterms. We get together, turn up on people's campaign
trails, and leave them completely screwed.

                              VLADIMIR PUTIN enters from the
                              darkness at the back of the
                              stage.

                         PUTIN
Do either of you have intention of getting on with show?
Some of us have important annex of nations to be doing
later.

                         CLINTON
You know, Vladimir. I often wonder why you did not choose
to help me instead of Donald. I was the better candidate.

                         PUTIN
We did offer. You deleted email we sent without reading it.

                         Beat.

                         CLINTON
Okay. Let us get on with the show.

                         PUTIN
Good.

                              PUTIN retreats back into the
                              darkness.

                         CLINTON
So has Donald Trump's political career died yet, Narrator?

                         NARRATOR
You'll need to come back at the end of the next act.

                                               (CONTINUED)

CONTINUED:

                              CLINTON
Then I will watch on from the wings waiting for my moment.
But can I stick around for just this bit? Only if you do
not mind?

                              NARRATOR

Well, I --

                              CLINTON
Great! I am sure that we will be the greatest of friends.
We already get along like... well, I do not really know. I
have never got on with anything before.
                    (beat)
Do continue.

                              NARRATOR

Thank you.
                    (to audience)
Though one fact cannot be disputed. While Donald may have
run off with his family to the America in the south, those
who now take his place in the Oval Office do so with no
couth.

                              CLINTON
That is right. There are some very bad people in there.
                    (leaning in)
And spoiler alert. It is Vladimir Putin and Sean Hannity. I
have read the script.

                              NARRATOR
Hillary, we're not supposed to tell them that much.

                              CLINTON
I am sorry. My mistake. I have never been that good at
knowing when I should leave.

                              NARRATOR

Now would be good.

                         CLINTON and the NARRATOR exit.

                                             (CONTINUED)

                                    Lights go up on THE OVAL OFFICE,
                                    where PUTIN sits with his feet
                                    on the desk while in front, SEAN
                                    HANNITY stands rehearsing.

                    HANNITY
                  (mid-rehearsal)
... And now, we come to our final story of the night, and
it's about those unpatriotic Democrats again. This time,
get this, they are going after our veterans. That's right,
those Democrats are calling for tougher sanctions on Russia
and the Russian people after everything they did fighting
alongside our boys in W-W-Two. Well, we here on Hannity
salute the sacrifices made by those brave Russian soldiers,
and we call upon the Democrats to start showing them the
respect they deserve.

                    PUTIN
Good. It be very good. I think it get message we want
across most well.

                    HANNITY
Thank you, Comrade Putin, sir.

                                    Footsteps grow in volume from
                                    offstage.

                    PUTIN
Quick. I think someone be coming. I should not be here.

                                    As HANNITY rushes to make
                                    himself look casual, PUTIN
                                    presses a small button on top of
                                    the desk. The entire desk, and
                                    PUTIN with it, swivels around to
                                    be replaced by an empty replica.

                                    ROBERT MUELLER enters carrying a
                                    file.

                    HANNITY
Mister Mueller. I wasn't expecting to see you here.

                                                        (CONTINUED)

                          MUELLER
I could say the same thing about yourself, Mister Hannity.
The Oval Office is, I do not believe, the Fox News studio.

                          HANNITY
Oh, well I was just --

                          MUELLER
Mister Hannity, do you know the current whereabouts of the
President?

                    Beat.

                          PUTIN (OFF)
                    (shouting out)
No, you do not.

                          HANNITY
                    (to MUELLER)
No, I do not.

                          MUELLER
I'm sorry?

                          HANNITY
No one knows where the President is right now.

                              MUELLER slams his file down on
                              the desk. The desk swivels back
                              around to reveal PUTIN, looking
                              shocked. MUELLER doesn't notice.

                          MUELLER
Mister Hannity, may I remind you that multiple eyewitnesses
claim that you were the last person to see the President
before his disappearance last month.

                              In a panic, PUTIN presses the
                              button and disappears again.

                          HANNITY
I have already testified under oath. I don't know anything.

                                             (CONTINUED)

                              MUELLER
I already know that you don't know anything, Mister
Hannity. But do you know where President Trump is?

                              HANNITY
No.

                         MUELLER picks his file up.

                              MUELLER
I hope that you're telling me the truth right now, Mister
Hannity. For your own sake.

                         He goes to leave but turns back
                         at the last moment.

                              MUELLER
Remember, Mister Hannity. I will be watching you. I am
always watching you.

                         MUELLER exits.

                              PUTIN (OFF)
                            (shouting out)
Is he gone?

                              HANNITY
He's gone.

                         The desk swivels back, and PUTIN
                         reappears.

                              PUTIN
Eyewitnesses? I thought we had all sent to gulag.

                              HANNITY
That's a very funny joke, Comrade Putin, sir.

                              PUTIN
I not joke. I never joke. But, you know, I actually be
getting tired of need to hide each time he come looking for
evidence. If I be honest, I actually be starting to miss
Donald.

                                        (CONTINUED)

                    HANNITY
So am I, Comrade Putin, sir.

                    PUTIN
And Donald was such good value. Whenever I needed laugh, I
just pick up phone and tell him foolish thing to do, and he
go and do it.

                    HANNITY
Very true, Comrade Putin, sir.

                              PUTIN stands and goes to put his
                              arm around HANNITY's shoulder.

                    PUTIN
Come now, Sean. You have not agree with all Putin says. It
almost me like something does bother you for past weeks.
Tell Putin what it be.

                    HANNITY
Well, this may sound dumb, but I'm worried that I might be
going to prison soon.

                    PUTIN
No. Of course, you not sound dumb. There be real chance you
be going to American gulag soon.

                    HANNITY
And if I only have a few months of freedom left, then I
don't want to spend them running for president. I want to
be around so that I can see Tucker Carlson grow into a real
boy.

                    PUTIN
I see. Well, perhaps it not be bad idea to bring back
Donald then. I be thinking of it for few days now. After
all, Fox and Friends have noticed he gone, and they notice
nothing.

                    HANNITY
It's a very good idea, Comrade Putin, sir.

                    PUTIN
Good. I be glad you agree. I leave you to get him them.

                                              (CONTINUED)

                         PUTIN goes to leave.

                         HANNITY
Me? But I don't know where he is.

                         PUTIN
Oh, Donald be in South America. He sent postcard.

                         HANNITY
South America?

                         PUTIN
Just follow trail of toilet paper that look like it once be
stuck to shoe bottom.

ACT III, SCENE THREE | THE TRUMP RANCH

                         The kitchen of a TRADITIONAL
                         SOUTH AMERICAN RANCH. A small
                         ramp leads to a raised area with
                         a table and refrigerator. Behind
                         them, the front door. At the
                         side of the scene, an open fire
                         where IVANKA TRUMP teaches ERIC
                         TRUMP math.

                         As South American folk music
                         plays in the background, the
                         NARRATOR enters.

                         NARRATOR
And so with the mission set out by Putin now a personal
goal for Sean Hannity, to South America he travels to bring
back to America the President to further the excruciation
of humanity.

But for the Trump family who Sean seeks to find, life has
changed, and just last week, a thirty-year lease on their
own ranch signed. And so the return of Donald is far from
set in stone, no matter the consequences for Hannity if the
President does not retake America's throne.

                                                   (CONTINUED)

>   The NARRATOR exits as the music
>   fades out.

                    IVANKA
Now tell me, what is four plus five?

                    ERIC
Nine?

                    IVANKA
No. It's six. Remember, we are in the Southern Hemisphere,
so everything is upside down.

>   DONALD TRUMP enters through the
>   front door.

                    TRUMP
You know, Eric Trump and Ivanka Trump, moving to South
America, was the very greatest decision that I, Donald J.
Trump, has ever made. This really is the life for us. Eric
Trump is finally learning to count to ten...

                    ERIC
One. Three. Two.

                    TRUMP
And I have just joined the local golf club. They said that
I had just enough money on me to cover the joining fee. It
was lucky I took that extra one million two hundred and
twenty-nine thousand four hundred and eleven with me.

                    ERIC
Nine. Eight.

                    TRUMP
Now, where is my greatest son, Donald Trump Junior?

                    IVANKA
He is working in his room, daddy.

                    TRUMP
I should shout for him to come here.
                    (shouting out)
Donald Trump Junior, come here.

                                              (CONTINUED)

>   DONALD TRUMP JUNIOR enters. He
>   is still tied to a chair from
>   the end of the previous act.

                    JUNIOR
Hey dad, I heard you shouting me.

                    TRUMP
Come here, Donald Trump Junior.

                    JUNIOR
Up there?

                    TRUMP
Yes. Up here, Donald Trump Junior. To the top of this ramp.

                    JUNIOR
Okay, you know, dad, it's really not easy for me to do that
right now. If you just untied me then --

                    TRUMP
I have already told you. I lost the key.

>   Slowly, JUNIOR uses his feet to
>   push the chair to the bottom of
>   the ramp and then slowly up it.

                    TRUMP
                (as JUNIOR approaches)
I need you to go and get my guitar for me, Donald Trump
Junior.

                    JUNIOR
Your guitar?

                    TRUMP
It is in my bedroom.

>   JUNIOR looks back down the ramp.

                    JUNIOR
You know what? Fine. I'll go get it.

                                              (CONTINUED)

>   JUNIOR makes his way back down
>   the ramp and exits as TRUMP
>   takes a seat at the table.

                              TRUMP
So, Eric Trump, what have you learned today?

                              ERIC
Four. Ten. Five. Seven. Six.

                              TRUMP
That is my social security number. How did you get that?
                         (beat)
Hey, Eric Trump, how rich am I?

                              ERIC
Jeff Bezos plus one Dollar.

                              TRUMP
What a great child.

>   JUNIOR returns, now with a
>   guitar. Everyone watches as he
>   makes his way back up the ramp.
>
>   At the top of the ramp, he hands
>   the guitar to TRUMP and joins
>   him at the table.

                              TRUMP
And now, I am going to play you all a great song. This is
going to be the greatest song performed by the greatest
person in the greatest way.

>   TRUMP coughs and strums the
>   guitar once.

                              TRUMP
/DO NOT CRY FOR ME, AMERICA./ Yeah!

>   TRUMP nods and looks pleased
>   with himself.

                                             (CONTINUED)

CONTINUED:

                    TRUMP
You are all supposed to clap. How about this one?

                         TRUMP coughs and strums the
                         guitar once more.

                    TRUMP
/IF I REALLY WERE A RICH MAN./ Yeah!

                         There is a sudden knock on the
                         door behind him.

                    TRUMP
That was not a clap.
                    (standing)
Quick. It might be Robert Mueller with questions. Ivanka
Trump, you need to hide. Eric Trump, you can stay here, we
can afford to lose you.

                         IVANKA rushes into the wings.

                    JUNIOR
And what about me, dad?

                         TRUMP grabs the back of JUNIOR's
                         chair and pushes him down the
                         ramp with enough force that he
                         continues offstage.

                    TRUMP
                    (to himself)
What about me? What about me? I know.

                         TRUMP stands by the door, puts
                         his hands over his face, and
                         then turns away from it.

                         Another knock.

                    TRUMP
                    (shouting out)
Beep. Donald J. Trump is not available at the moment.
Please leave a message for Donald J. Trump after the
beep... Bing, bing, bong, bong.

                                             (CONTINUED)

                         Another knock.

                    TRUMP
Okay. Plan number B.
                    (shouting out)
We are not here. No one is here.

                         Another knock.

                    TRUMP
This will be okay. It will be okay.

                         Cautiously, TRUMP turns back to
                         the door and pulls back the
                         curtain to see who is there.

                    IVANKA
                    (returning)
Who is it, daddy?

                    TRUMP
Sean Hannity.

                         ERIC screams as TRUMP lets the
                         curtain fall back down.

                    ERIC
Sorry. I thought you said a vampire.

                         Another knock.

                    TRUMP
Quick. Hide. It might be Robert Mueller --

                    IVANKA
It's Sean Hannity, daddy.

                    TRUMP
How do you know?

                    IVANKA
You just said it was.

                                             (CONTINUED)

CONTINUED:

>   TRUMP opens the door, and
>   HANNITY enters, looking as
>   though he's faced a long
>   journey.

                    HANNITY
I am so glad that I've found you, sir. I've been looking
for the right place for days.

>   TRUMP stares at HANNITY without
>   showing any emotion.

                    TRUMP
Sean Hannity.

                    HANNITY
Mister President, sir. You have no idea how good it is to
see you again.

                    TRUMP
Sean Hannity, it is always good to see me.

>   JUNIOR returns.

                    JUNIOR
Is it safe?

                    HANNITY
And Junior, you're here too.
                    (to IVANKA)
And get this, Ivanka too. I'm so glad to find the three of
you here.
                    (to ERIC)
And Eric.

                    IVANKA
Hello, Sean. You are honored to meet my father again.

>   TRUMP gestures for HANNITY to
>   take his attention away from
>   IVANKA.

                    TRUMP
I am here, Sean Hannity. I am not over there.

                                            (CONTINUED)

                         HANNITY
I'm sorry, Mister President. I didn't mean to give you any
undivided attention.

                                   JUNIOR begins to make his way
                                   back up the ramp as TRUMP sits
                                   at the table and gestures for
                                   HANNITY to do the same.

                         TRUMP
So what can I do for you, Sean Hannity?
                    (to JUNIOR)
Donald Trump Junior, fetch me a diet cola.

                         JUNIOR
Where are they?

                         TRUMP
They are in the refrigerator.

                                   JUNIOR begins to move closer to
                                   the refrigerator as...

                         TRUMP
Not that refrigerator. I have my own private Presidential
refrigerator in my bedroom. It is so cold. It is the most
coldest refrigerator ever. Even standing close to it makes
you deny global warming and causes all of your nipples to
go as hard as entry to Trump University.

                         JUNIOR
Do I have to go?

                         TRUMP
Yes. I have to talk to Sean Hannity.

                                   JUNIOR makes his way back down
                                   the ramp and exits once more.

                         TRUMP
So what can I do for you, Sean Hannity?

                         HANNITY
Well, Mister President, sir, I've come to take you home.

                                                      (CONTINUED)

TRUMP
But I am home. This is my home, Sean Hannity.

HANNITY
I meant your real home, sir. The United States of America.
You're our President, sir. And we need you back.

TRUMP
I am sorry, Sean Hannity, but I am not coming back. This is
my home now. It is so great. We have got our life set out.
I have even ordered a no foreign immigrants sign for the
front door. I wanted to own Jeff Bezos, so instead of
Amazon, I ordered it from el Amazonas.

HANNITY
But, Mister President, we need you. I need you. I can get
away with so much more while you're around. And America
needs you to come and save us all from the Democrats and
the liberals. Who knows where the next big threat might
come from? It could be from electronic cigarettes. We are
going to need your leadership to protect us from things
that could kill literally six of us. We need to leave here,
break Jared out of prison, get back to the Oval Office, and
get back to work.

IVANKA
(with lust)
Jared?

TRUMP
He did not say Jared Kushner. He said... Jobs. Many jobs. I
have created so many jobs. Good jobs. A lot of distracting
jobs. Jobs. Yeah!

                    ERIC applauds.

TRUMP
Thank you, Eric Trump.

                         JUNIOR returns with a can of
                         diet cola and begins making his
                         way back up the ramp.

                                                  (CONTINUED)

                         HANNITY
And you could create so many more jobs, Mister President.
Get this. You could truly make America great again.

                         TRUMP
Are you saying that I have not already made America great
again, Sean Hannity? I am the greatest President ever. I
had Siri read to me from Twitter that since people have
thought I left the country, I have the highest approval
ratings ever.

                         HANNITY
I meant that you could make America great again, again. You
could be the greatest ever Donald J. Trump.

                              As JUNIOR makes his way to the
                              top of the ramp, he drops the
                              can, and it rolls back down.

                         TRUMP
I am sorry, Sean Hannity.
                    (to JUNIOR)
Go and get that can, Donald Trump Junior.
                    (to HANNITY)
But I do not want to come back.

                         JUNIOR
Make Eric get it.

                         TRUMP
Eric Trump, get that can from the floor.

                              ERIC stands and walks over to
                              the can.

                         TRUMP
                    (to HANNITY)
I like my life here, Sean Hannity. No one wants to ask me
questions and there are no Russians to blackmail me.

                         HANNITY
Some would say that it's your constitutional duty to
return, Mister President.

                                                  (CONTINUED)

                         ERIC opens the can, and it
                         sprays in his face.

                    TRUMP
Eric Trump, go and get another diet cola.
               (to HANNITY)
I do not know a mister constitution, Sean Hannity.

                    ERIC
Make Junior go and get it.

                    TRUMP
Donald Trump Junior, go and get another diet cola.
               (to HANNITY)
The only way I would ever return is if we run out of diet
cola or anything like that.

                    JUNIOR
I can't get another. That was the last one.
               (beat)
We don't have any regular cola either, or anything like
that.

                         Beat.

                    TRUMP
Sean Hannity, I have reconsidered. So long as I get to fly
in first-class and they serve fried chicken on the plane, I
will come home.

                    HANNITY
I'm sorry to let you down, Mister President. But we can't
fly back. Robert Mueller and his team still want to
question you, and they might be waiting at the airport.

                    TRUMP
What are you suggesting?

                    HANNITY
We'll have to make our way back to Washington unnoticed. We
have to journey north to Mexico and then cross the border
on foot.

                                        (CONTINUED)

CONTINUED:

                    JUNIOR
You mean, we have to walk?

                    HANNITY
It's the only option we've got.

                    TRUMP
Can we stop for fried chicken on the way?

                    ERIC
Can I get a toy with mine?

                    TRUMP
And Eric Trump will have a toy with his.

                    HANNITY
I'm sure that we'll be able to find food, Mister President.

                    TRUMP
                 (standing)
Okay, Ivanka Trump, I want you to stay close to me so that
we do not lose you. Donald Trump Junior, I want you to keep
an eye on Eric Trump and try to lose him.

                              ERIC runs to hug JUNIOR at the
                              top of the ramp.

                    ERIC
Yay! Road trip buddy.

                              As ERIC releases JUNIOR, he
                              knocks him back down the ramp
                              and offstage.

                    JUNIOR
                 (returning)
You know, dad? I think this would be a lot easier if I
weren't still tied to this chair.

                              TRUMP reaches into his pocket
                              and pulls out a small key which
                              he uses to untie JUNIOR.

                                        (CONTINUED)

CONTINUED:

                         JUNIOR
I thought you said that you'd lost the key?

                         TRUMP
I did say that I had lost the key.

                         JUNIOR
Then why have you just pulled it out of your pocket?

                         TRUMP
I found it again.

                    Beat.

                         IVANKA
Daddy, what are you going to do about Kellyanne? She isn't
home yet.

                         TRUMP
I will leave her a note.

                              TRUMP goes to the table to
                              scribble on a piece of paper.

                         HANNITY
Is there anything I can do, Mister Trump?

                              TRUMP looks at HANNITY.

                         TRUMP
Sean Hannity, I have a special job for you.

ACT III, SCENE FOUR | THE BORDER CROSSING

                              A BORDER CROSSING point between
                              Mexico and the United States
                              where DMITRY SUREFIRE and PETROV
                              SUREFIRE stand either side of a
                              door marked "door to the United
                              States."

                                              (CONTINUED)

                         NARRATOR
                        (entering)
With Hannity succeeding in talking around his friend to
make him feel about a return convinced, the President and
his party set off home to ensure once more that the nation
is winced.

But before setting foot on his kingdom's land, there are
issues to arise for Donald from earlier policies that were
not well planned. For he, his family, and Sean Hannity, it
does not matter what their personal vanity, their hopes of
returning without issue to American ground are all soon to
be drowned.

                    The NARRATOR exits.

                         DMITRY
Do you think new job we have is promotion, Petrov?

                         PETROV
I do, Dmitry.

                         DMITRY
I applied for Space Force, but they rejected me.

                         PETROV
Space Force? Why apply for Space Force?

                         DMITRY
I want to go into space, Petrov.

                         PETROV
We need not join Space Force to visit space, Dmitry. We be
Russian. Russia own space. We go to space whenever we want.

                         DMITRY
Can we go now? It be better than standing here.

                    PETROV looks at him, worried.

                         PETROV
Speak cautious, Dmitry. Boss may be listening to us. And
besides, I think Comrade Putin know what he be doing when
he place us here. We have essential job, no?

                                        (CONTINUED)

CONTINUED:

                              DMITRY
What job?

                              PETROV
We have to guard America against the bad people.

                              DMITRY
What do you mean the bad people?

                              PETROV
I mean all the bad people, Dmitry. The criminals. The
conmen. The rapists.

                    HANNITY enters carrying TRUMP on
                    his shoulders.

                              HANNITY
I think we've made it, Mister President.

                              TRUMP
I think I can smell the freedom, Sean Hannity.

                              DMITRY
Oh, the bad people. I know what you mean, Petrov.

                    TRUMP climbs down as IVANKA
                    enters, followed by JUNIOR, who
                    holds the end of a children's
                    walking harness worn by ERIC.

                              TRUMP
                          (to the group)
I will handle this.

                    As TRUMP approaches the door,
                    DMITRY and PETROV step in to
                    block him.

                    TRUMP walks back casually, and
                    they step aside. A moment later,
                    TRUMP turns back to them, and
                    they step in once more.

                                            (CONTINUED)

CONTINUED:

                    TRUMP
               (to the group)
Someone else handle this.

                         IVANKA now steps forward. As
                         with her father, DMITRY and
                         PETROV stand in to block her.

                    IVANKA
Hello. You are both honored to meet my father today. Can we
all please come in?

                    PETROV
There be no entry.

                    DMITRY
We not let anyone in.

                         JUNIOR steps forward.

                    JUNIOR
But we are American citizens. And not just citizens. We are
natural-born citizens. Me, my father, my sister, Sean
Hannity, all of us natural born. And Eric...
               (beat)
He's an American.

                    ERIC
I wee freedom showers.

                    PETROV
But do you have papers in correct order?

                    DMITRY
Anyone could claim they are American. But can you prove it?

                    HANNITY
               (to TRUMP)
Why don't we just go around the side of the door, Mister
President? They can't guard everywhere.

                    TRUMP
We cannot go around it, Sean Hannity. There is a wall. A
great big wall. I built it.

                                             (CONTINUED)

> HANNITY leans to look at either
> side of the door.

                    HANNITY
Mister President, sir. There is no wall. I can see that
there isn't. No wall has been built here.

                    TRUMP
Are you calling me a liar, Sean Hannity?

                    HANNITY
No, Mister President. I was just pointing out that --

                    TRUMP
Sean Hannity, stop right there, or I will have to report
this to Comrade Putin.

> DMITRY and PETROV look worried.

                    JUNIOR
                (to DMITRY and PETROV)
You know, we know Comrade Putin personally. He wouldn't be
happy if he knew you weren't letting us in.

                    PETROV
We are under instructions not to let anyone through.

                    HANNITY
                (stepping forward)
You want papers? Take these papers.

> HANNITY takes a pile of bills
> from his pocket and hands them
> to DMITRY and PETROV.

                    HANNITY
Can we come through now?

> DMITRY and PETROV step aside to
> let them through the door.

                    TRUMP
Did you see my negotiating? Did you all see how great I
was? That was some great negotiating.

                                              (CONTINUED)

                         HANNITY
You did very well, Mister President.

                              DMITRY and PETROV begin to count
                              the bills.

                         DMITRY
This is real money, Petrov.

                         PETROV
Real United States Dollar, Dmitry.

                         HANNITY
                    (hanging back)
Hey, those aren't just United States Dollars. Those are
freedom bucks.

ACT III, SCENE FIVE | BREAKING KUSHNER OUT

                              From the depths of a dark stage,
                              a single voice shouts out.

                    COHEN (IN DARKNESS)
                    (shouting out)
Hello. I want to see the manager. The boss. This is not
what I signed up for.

                              A spotlight shines upon a PRISON
                              CELL where MICHAEL COHEN sits on
                              a bed.

                         COHEN
                    (shouting out)
I was told that if I flipped on boss Trump, then I'd get a
light sentence. This is no light sentence. I didn't sign up
to be sharing no cell with this guy.

                              A second spotlight shines upon
                              JARED KUSHNER, who sits in the
                              corner of the cell rocking.

                                             (CONTINUED)

                          KUSHNER
                    (muttering to himself)
I don't know... I want my mommy... where the President
is... I'm innocent... I don't know anything... It wasn't
Mister Trump or me... Ivanka... I want my mommy...

                          NARRATOR
                        (entering)
The border crossed eventually and back onto the soil of
their home nation, but still, there's work to be done as
another waits to be broken out on permanent probation.

                    KUSHNER sobs loudly.

                          COHEN
                      (shouting out)
Oh, great. And now he's crying again. Can't a felon get no
peace around these parts?

                          NARRATOR
For in a cell sits crying advisor Jared Kushner, and for
company, former lawyer Michael Cohen. The earlier here for
refusing to talk the truth about Trump, which all know he
is all-knowing.

                              The NARRATOR exits as other
                              voices begin to come from the
                              opposite wing.

                          HANNITY (OFF)
I think we just have to take a left here, Mister President.
And then this should be the corridor to the cells.

                          TRUMP (OFF)
Okay, Sean Hannity. So, here is my great plan.
                        (beat)
Donald Trump Junior, tell us what my great plan is.

                          JUNIOR (OFF)
Okay, so here is what is going to happen. Dad, Sean, you're
both going to try the door to the cell and use strength to
break it down. I'm going to go up into the ceiling and then
lower myself down into the cell from above.

                                              (CONTINUED)

                         ERIC (OFF)
I'm going to push this button.

                              Flashing lights and alarms fill
                              the stage.

                         JUNIOR (OFF)
Turn it off.

                              The lights and alarms stop.

                         TRUMP (OFF)
Donald Trump Junior, take Eric Trump with you.

                         JUNIOR (OFF)
Fine. But keep Ivanka with you.

                         TRUMP (OFF)
Okay.

                              Offstage there is the sound of
                              movement followed by silence.

                         HANNITY (OFF)
Hold on, Mister President. I think I've found the light
switch.

                         TRUMP (OFF)
How do you know, Sean Hannity?

                              The stage lights up.

                         HANNITY
Because it turned the lights on.

                         COHEN
                    (shouting out)
Hey, what's going on? I don't remember asking for no light.

                              HANNITY, IVANKA and TRUMP enter.

                              Noticing KUSHNER, IVANKA runs up
                              to the bars of the cell as he
                              looks up at her.

                                             (CONTINUED)

                    IVANKA
                 (lovingly)
Jared.

                         KUSHNER stands and approaches
                         IVANKA. For a moment, they gaze
                         into each other's eyes.

                    IVANKA
You are honored to be broken out of jail by my father
today.

                    TRUMP
                 (to HANNITY)
Do we really need Jared Kushner?

                         KUSHNER reaches into his pocket
                         and pulls out paper and a pen,
                         which he uses to begin writing.

                    HANNITY
I think so, Mister President. We've come this far.

                         KUSHNER hands the paper to
                         IVANKA.

                    IVANKA
                 (reading)
"I love you, Ivanka. But your father tricked me and told me
to wait for him in the Oval Office."
                 (to KUSHNER)
Oh, that is just my father's sense of humor.
                 (reading)
"The F-B-I came looking for him so they could ask him some
questions. Instead, they arrested me because I wouldn't
talk."

                         COHEN stands and approaches.

                    COHEN
You know, speaking of questions, I've got a few. What are
you all doing here? I don't want to be involved with you
guys no more.
                    (MORE)

                                             (CONTINUED)

CONTINUED:

                         COHEN (CONT'D)
Also, does anyone know what time they're bringing the snack
cart around? I'd love some potato chips right about now.

                         TRUMP
                    (to HANNITY)
Sean Hannity, who is this man?

                         HANNITY
It's Michael Cohen, Mister President. He was your lawyer.

                    TRUMP turns to COHEN.

                         TRUMP
I do not know you. I have never met you.

                         COHEN
I know you, though, boss. You're a bad man.

                         HANNITY
                    (to TRUMP)
We should be getting on with breaking Jared out before a
guard comes along.

                              TRUMP attempts to open the cell
                              door, but it doesn't open.

                         TRUMP
It is not opening, Sean Hannity. It must be rigged.

                              TRUMP tries once more, this time
                              with more force. Failing again,
                              he watches HANNITY walk over and
                              open it easily on his first try.

                         TRUMP
Close the door, Sean Hannity.

                              HANNITY closes the door.

                              TRUMP grabs the handle and leans
                              against the door. It opens, and
                              he falls forward into the cell.

                                             (CONTINUED)

CONTINUED:

                         TRUMP
That was easy.

                         COHEN
It's supposed to be easy. It's so the guards can get in if
they need to.

                                   From the top of the stage,
                                   JUNIOR begins to be lowered into
                                   the cell on a rope.

                         JUNIOR
Any luck on that side?

                         TRUMP
I have got it open, Donald Trump Junior.

                                   JUNIOR reaches the ground and
                                   unties himself from the rope.

                         JUNIOR
                     (shouting up)
Hey, buddy, father's got it open. You can come down now.

                         ERIC (OFF)
Okay.

                         JUNIOR
                     (to TRUMP)
So, how did you do it, dad?

                         TRUMP
I used great skill and great strength.

                                   At the top of the stage, ERIC's
                                   head appears, followed by his
                                   body, as he is lowered upside
                                   down with his rope tied to just
                                   one ankle.

                         ERIC
Hey, Junior, all of my blood is rushing to my head. I'm
going to look like dad soon.

                                                    (CONTINUED)

CONTINUED:

                    TRUMP
You do not have any blood, Eric Trump.

                    ERIC
Hey, Junior, was I supposed to tie the other end of the
rope to something first?

                              Beat, and then ERIC falls the
                              final few feet before the other
                              end of the rope follows.

                    TRUMP
Why is it so cold in here?

                    COHEN
There's an open window at the end of the corridor.

                    TRUMP
I know how to fix this.

                         TRUMP goes to close the door.

                    COHEN/ HANNITY/ IVANKA/ JUNIOR
NO!

                              KUSHNER holds up a piece of
                              paper with "NO!" written on it
                              as the door closes.

                    TRUMP
Why is it still cold?

                    COHEN
Because the cell is made out of metal bars with gaps in
between them.

                    TRUMP
We should just go somewhere warmer then.

                              TRUMP attempts to open the door
                              again but fails.

                    TRUMP
Why won't it open, Sean Hannity?

                                             (CONTINUED)

CONTINUED:

                        HANNITY
I think it only opens from the outside, Mister President.
                    (to JUNIOR)
Can we get out the way you came in?

                                    JUNIOR pulls on the rope he was
                                    lowered in on. It falls to the
                                    ground.

                        JUNIOR
Eric, did you forget to tie the end of both ropes?

                                    Beat, and then they all turn to
                                    look at ERIC who is stuck with
                                    his head in the bars.

                        ERIC
My head hurts.

ACT III, SCENE SIX | BACK IN THE OVAL OFFICE

                                    A dark stage except for a single
                                    centered spotlight into which
                                    the NARRATOR enters.

                        NARRATOR
And so five become six as Kushner takes his place back in
the occult. But before plans can continue, they must return
to the White House for there is another with whom they all
must consult.

Further too, more old friends die hard, and they're ready
to return to fight the fight against each every nationwide
liberal at heart. While upon their mater's fleeing they
worried first for their own well-being, with the
President's return now so imminent --

                                    MIKE PENCE enters wearing a
                                    leather jacket and carrying a
                                    carton of milk.

                                                        (CONTINUED)

CONTINUED:

                              PENCE
Mister President, I'm back, sir. I have the milk you asked
for.

                                        PENCE notices the NARRATOR is
                                        alone.

                              PENCE
Oh, is the President not here?

                              NARRATOR
He's not got back yet.

                              PENCE
I'll come back soon then.

                              NARRATOR
Where have you been?

                              PENCE
I went to fetch some milk

                              NARRATOR
For a month?

                              PENCE
It's good milk.

                                        PENCE turns to exit, revealing
                                        as he does that the back of his
                                        jacket is embossed with an "I
                                        LOVE VEGAS" slogan.

                                        As PENCE exits, the NARRATOR
                                        turns their attention back to
                                        the audience.

                              NARRATOR
While upon their master's fleeing, they worried first for
their own well-being, with the President's return now so
imminent, so are loyalties and a following ever equally non-
discriminant.

                                                        (CONTINUED)

                              THE NARRATOR exits as lights go
                              up on the OVAL OFFICE, where
                              PUTIN sits alone with his feet
                              up on the desk.

                              To one side stands a large crate
                              covered in mailing stickers.

                              ERIC, HANNITY, IVANKA, JUNIOR,
                              KUSHNER, and TRUMP enter.

                         TRUMP
Who would ever have thought that a get out of jail free
card would have actually worked?

                         JUNIOR
You know, it's lucky that those guards had lost the one
from their set.

                              PUTIN stands and approaches.

                         PUTIN
                        (drawn out)
Donald...

                              TRUMP flinches as PUTIN hugs
                              him.

                         PUTIN
It be good to have you back. Now dance for Putin.

                         TRUMP
I do not want to dance.

                         PUTIN
I said dance.

                              TRUMP begins to dance on the
                              spot.

                         PUTIN
It be just like old time. You can stop now.

                              TRUMP stops dancing.

                                             (CONTINUED)

CONTINUED:

                         PUTIN
                    (to HANNITY)
You did work good.

                         HANNITY
Thank you, Comrade Putin, sir.

                         PUTIN
                    (to TRUMP)
So, Donald. With you back, I think it be time that we
increase moves to take control of all America, no?

                    PUTIN returns to the desk.

                         TRUMP
I thought I made the decisions around here?

                    As he sits, PUTIN shakes his
                    head.

                         PUTIN
No.
                    (to HANNITY)
Sean, go back to Fox News and wait for instruction.

                         HANNITY
Yes, sir.

                    HANNITY bows and exits.

                         IVANKA
                    (to PUTIN)
Daddy, can Jared and I have some free time to catch up?

                         TRUMP
Of --

                         PUTIN
                    (to IVANKA)
Yes, you may.

                    TRUMP looks at PUTIN and then to
                    IVANKA.

                                             (CONTINUED)

                         TRUMP
I though that --

                    IVANKA and KUSHNER exit.

                         PUTIN
Now, Donald. Before we get down to business.
                    (gesturing at the crate)
This package came for you earlier.

                    TRUMP approaches the crate.

                         TRUMP
What is it?

                         PUTIN
It be big box. But I hear voices from inside earlier.

                         TRUMP
                    (to crate)
Hello.

                    A beat, and then a muffled voice
                    comes from within the crate.

                    CONWAY (IN CRATE)
Mister Trump, is that you?

                         TRUMP
                    (to crate)
Hello.

                    PUTIN grabs a crowbar from under
                    the desk and uses it on the
                    crate. The front falls open to
                    reveal KELLYANNE CONWAY stuck
                    upside down.

                         PUTIN
I not be expecting that.

                         CONWAY
Is it safe to come out now?

                                        (CONTINUED)

CONTINUED:

                         PUTIN
It be safe.

                    CONWAY falls out of the crate.

                         CONWAY
                       (standing up)
I got your note, Mister Trump.

                         TRUMP
Hello, Kellyanne Conway.

                         CONWAY
Mister President. I am ready to serve at your pleasure once
more.

                    CONWAY goes to bow but loses her
                    balance and falls over.

                         PUTIN
Perhaps she need moment.

                         JUNIOR
You know, I was expecting something more impressive.

                         PUTIN
What do you want Putin to do? Put her back in box and rig
door with firework for second opening? Order parade? No.
Kellyanne got left behind so got shipped because ride share
app not go that far. What you expect? She came out of box
because box be what she in. It be simple.

                         TRUMP
But --

                         PUTIN
Donald. Shut up.

                    Approaching footsteps come from
                    offstage.

                         PUTIN
We all need hide. Now.

                                             (CONTINUED)

CONTINUED:

                              All panicking, CONWAY returns to
                              the crate as JUNIOR goes to hide
                              behind a curtain, and ERIC moves
                              to the wall and sticks a nearby
                              lampshade on his head.

                    TRUMP
What do I do?

                    PUTIN
Come here.

                              TRUMP joins PUTIN at the desk,
                              the later pushing the button for
                              them to swivel around.

                              MUELLER enters and looks around.

                    MUELLER
                 (to himself)
It seems different in here. I'm sure I just heard voices
too. And there is something funny in the air.
                 (sniffing)
The smell of cheap cologne, fried chicken, South East
Florida, and the third cubicle along in the bathroom of a
Tuscaloosa fast food place at closing on the day of a kid's
birthday party.

                              MUELLER walks over to a window
                              and opens the curtain next to
                              the one where JUNIOR is hidden.

                    MUELLER
Why's it so dark in here?

                              MUELLER looks over and points at
                              the lampshade on ERIC's head.

                    MUELLER
Someone should get that light looked at. I've never seen
one looking so dim.

                              MUELLER takes a final look
                              around.

                                                   (CONTINUED)

                         MUELLER
Well, it doesn't look like there's any Trumps in here. I'll
try the fast-food restaurants.

                         MUELLER exits.

                         They wait for a moment before
                         coming out from their hiding
                         places. ERIC walks forward with
                         the lampshade stuck on his head.

                         ERIC
Can I get some help here?

                         JUNIOR
I'm coming, buddy.

                         JUNIOR goes to help ERIC.

                         TRUMP
                    (to PUTIN)
How long has the desk done that?

                         PUTIN
Ever since you leave. I had feature put in so I can easily
hide when people come with question.

                         TRUMP
Can I have a go?

                         PUTIN
If you must.

                         TRUMP pushes the button on the
                         desk, and he and PUTIN swivel.

                         TRUMP (OFF)
I want to get one of these.

                         They swivel back.

                         PUTIN
This be yours.

                                        (CONTINUED)

CONTINUED:

                              TRUMP
I want to press it again.

                              PUTIN
Donald.

                    TRUMP presses the button again,
                    and they swivel back out of
                    sight. A moment later, they
                    return. TRUMP presses it again,
                    and again, and again.

                              PUTIN
DONALD!

                    The next time the desk comes
                    back around, PUTIN and TRUMP are
                    replaced by CLINTON.

                              CLINTON
Ah. Ha. Ha. Ha. I told you. I told you that it would
happen, and none of you believed me. But here I am. My
rightful home. Hillary Rodham Clinton in the Oval Office.
This is how it should be. I have dreamt of this moment. I
am the Presid --

                    The desk swivels back to PUTIN
                    and TRUMP.

                              CLINTON (OFF)
No. This is my moment.

                    The desk swivels back to CLINTON
                    and then back and forth between
                    her and PUTIN and TRUMP before
                    stopping on CLINTON.

                              CLINTON
No one can take this moment away from me.

                    The desk swivels back...

                                                  (CONTINUED)

                          CLINTON
                       (disappearing)
Oh. It turns out they can.

                              ... this time to TRUMP and PENCE
                              who still holding the milk.

                              Beat.

                          PENCE
I got that milk you asked me to fetch, Mister President.

                              PENCE and TRUMP stand and move
                              to one side.

                              The desk swivels once more, and
                              PUTIN returns.

                          PUTIN
You know, I think that desk really need putting on slower
setting.

                          TRUMP
                       (to PENCE)
It is good to see you again, Mike Pence.

                          PENCE
I have missed you, Mister President, sir.

                          PUTIN
Okay, yes. There be time to catch up later. We have work
now.

                          PENCE
I do apologize. Do continue.

                              PUTIN moves back to the desk.

                          PUTIN
Good. So, I be thinking. We need effort to secure way of
ensuring our regime continue for long-term.

                          PENCE
What did you have in mind, Comrade?

                                        (CONTINUED)

CONTINUED:

                              PUTIN
Supreme Court. It be time we get a new pick for Donald
before he be impeached.

                              PENCE
But there isn't a vacancy?

                              PUTIN
Oh. Not worry about small matter like that. Putin has plan
for that. Putin always have plan.
                         (to TRUMP)
Donald, I have other work I must do now. But before I
leave, dance one more time for Putin.

                              TRUMP
I do not want to dance.

                              PUTIN
I said dance.

                         TRUMP performs a short dance on
                         the spot.

                              PUTIN
Such good value.

                         PUTIN presses the button on the
                         desk, and he disappears to be
                         replaced by the NARRATOR.

                              NARRATOR
                         (walking forward)
And so back together are Trump and friends ready to stamp
down more authority, all with the aid of Putin's new plan
for further control now being an administration priority.

But playing most on the mind of Donald and the rest, a
problem to which half can now attest. For an insecure
border is what they believe sits on the country's southern
end, but luckily for the President, it is a matter to which
Mike Pence and Kellyanne Conway have plans to attend.

                         The NARRATOR exits.

                                             (CONTINUED)

                         PENCE
Mister President, sir, you may remember, before your
departure, you were discussing ways to secure the border.

                         TRUMP
I want to build a great big wall, Mike Pence.

                         PENCE
Well, sir, Kellyanne Conway and I would like to show you
some prototypes that we were working on before you left.

                         TRUMP
Did Mexico pay for them?

                         PENCE
No. They said they wouldn't.

                         TRUMP
Then who did pay for them?

                         CONWAY
No one paid for them, Mister President. We paid ourselves.

                         TRUMP
I cannot have that, Kellyanne Conway. If Mexico refuses to
pay for them, then someone else should.
                    (to JUNIOR)
Donald Trump Junior, did you pay any tax last year?

                         JUNIOR
No. Not me.

                         TRUMP
Eric Trump, did you pay any tax last year?

                         ERIC
I run away before they can tell me what the fare is.

                         TRUMP
Mike Pence, did you pay any tax last year?

                         PENCE
I am officially a church for tax purposes, sir.

                                        (CONTINUED)

                              TRUMP
Kellyanne Conway, did you pay any tax last year?

                              CONWAY
Yes, I did.

                              TRUMP
I need to borrow money.

                              CONWAY
How much do you need?

                              TRUMP
I'll check.
                         (to PENCE)
Mike Pence, how much did you and Kellyanne Conway spend to
build the wall?

                              PENCE
Ten thousand dollars, sir.

                              TRUMP
                         (to CONWAY)
Kellyanne Conway, I need to borrow twenty thousand dollars.

                              CONWAY
Sure thing, Mister President.

                                   CONWAY pulls a checkbook out of
                                   her pocket, writes a check and
                                   hands it to TRUMP.

                              CONWAY
Just make sure I get it back.

                                   TRUMP rips the check in two and
                                   pockets one half.

                              TRUMP
                         (to PENCE)
Mike Pence, I have found someone to give you ten thousand
dollars to cover the wall.

                                                        (CONTINUED)

CONTINUED:

                         PENCE
That is very kind of you, Mister President.

                              TRUMP hands PENCE the other half
                              of the check.

                         PENCE
And here is your five thousand dollars, Kellyanne.

                              PENCE rips the half check in two
                              and hands one piece to CONWAY.

                         CONWAY
You're very kind, Mike.

                         TRUMP
Now show me these walls.

                         PENCE
Kellyanne, could you fetch the first prototype, please?

                         CONWAY exits.

                         PENCE
So this is our first idea, Mister Trump.

                              CONWAY enters pulling along a
                              wooden fence, with a door in the
                              middle, mounted on wheels.

                         TRUMP
What is it, Mike Pence?

                         PENCE
It is a wooden fence, Mister President.

                         JUNIOR
It's got a door in the middle of it.

                         TRUMP
Why has it got a door in the middle of it?

                                              (CONTINUED)

                         CONWAY
The door is there so that we can open it to kick all of the
bad people out of our country.

                         JUNIOR
But doesn't that mean that bad people can also come into
the country?

                         PENCE
I offer you my assurances, the door does not allow any --

                              The door opens, and the NARRATOR
                              walks through.

                         PENCE
Kellyanne, I think that we may have to reconsider the
wooden fence.

                              CONWAY exits with the fence.

                         NARRATOR
Ever predictable was the failure of Conway and Pence's
first wooden attempt, but no matter, for a second they have
with far fewer splinters, though with a chance of growing
unkempt.

                              The NARRATOR exits as CONWAY
                              enters pulling along a large
                              hedge on wheels.

                         PENCE
This is our second idea.

                         TRUMP
What is it?

                         PENCE
It is a hedge, Mister President.

                         CONWAY
We are proposing to build a border hedge. It's a more
environmentally friendly option.

                                                  (CONTINUED)

                         TRUMP
I do not like environmentally friendly, Kellyanne Conway.

                         JUNIOR
Could we get it made out of plastic in China?

                         CONWAY
Yes, we could. And look at the benefits of the design.
There is no door.

                                        The NARRATOR enters with a
                                        chainsaw which they use to cut
                                        through the hedge.

                         PENCE
I'm not so sure about the hedge, Kellyanne. Bring out our
third idea.

                                        CONWAY exits with the hedge.

                         NARRATOR
Green though it may be, their second idea fails to show
bloom, while even for their third that waits in the wings,
even there for improvements, there still exists room.

                                        The NARRATOR exits as CONWAY
                                        enters pulling along a brick
                                        wall on wheels.

                         PENCE
And this is our third idea, Mister President.

                         CONWAY
It's brick. Solid brick. No door and no way to cut through.

                                        The NARRATOR enters with a
                                        ladder which they use to climb
                                        to the top of the wall.

                         PENCE
We forgot about ladders, Mister President.

                                        The NARRATOR climbs back down.

                                                       (CONTINUED)

CONTINUED:

PENCE
Kellyanne, do you have our fourth prototype ready?

CONWAY
It's ready.

> CONWAY exits with the brick
> wall.

NARRATOR
And so even solid brick is not a solution that is bestowed
by Trump an honored tick. But one final idea they have
ready to show, and it's one that can be painful for those
who get close without the know.

> CONWAY enters pulling along an
> electric fence on wheels.

PENCE
Now this, Mister President. This is an electric fence.

CONWAY
(to the NARRATOR)
Go on. Try your metal chainsaw or your metal ladder now.

> The NARRATOR approaches the
> fence with caution.

NARRATOR
Eric, come here.

> ERIC walks over to the NARRATOR,
> who whispers in his ear.

ERIC
Okay.

> ERIC closes his eyes, sticks out
> his tongue, and then moves
> slowly closer toward the fence.

> The entire room goes dark with a
> loud ban.

(CONTINUED)

                         ERIC (IN DARKNESS)
You said it tasted like candy.

                         NARRATOR
                    (to CONWAY)
No, it works.

                         TRUMP
Mike Pence, Kellyanne Conway, this is a very good idea. But
it needs one small change to make it a very great idea.

                         PENCE
What do you suggest, Mister President?

                         TRUMP
Electric is for liberals. They are not so smart. But I am
smart. I do not want electric. I want coal.

                    Beat.

                         PENCE
You want a coal fence?

                         TRUMP

Correct.

                         PENCE
Kellyanne?

                         CONWAY
                    (to TRUMP)
Sir, I'm not sure that what you're suggesting would
actually be possible.

                         TRUMP
Make it possible.

                         CONWAY and PENCE look at each
                         other for a brief moment.

                         PENCE
We will try our best, Mister President.

                                                  (CONTINUED)

CONTINUED:

                    TRUMP
Good. Now I need to go on executive time. There are a lot
of important things I need to do.
                    (to JUNIOR)
Donald Trump Junior, take Eric Trump for a walk so that he
can go toilet.
                    (to CONWAY)
Kellyanne Conway, go and make me a coal fence.
                    (to PENCE)
Mike Pence.

                    PENCE
I'm at your service, sir.

                              CONWAY exits with the electric
                              fence as ERIC, JUNIOR, and the
                              NARRATOR follow.

                    TRUMP
I need you to go and mail a letter for me.

                              TRUMP picks up a small golden
                              envelope from the desk.

                    TRUMP
This is for my good friend, Kim Jong-Un.

                              TRUMP hands PENCE the envelope.

                    TRUMP
The envelope is not small. My hands are just <u>huge</u>.

                    PENCE
I will make sure that this gets where it needs to go,
Mister President.

                    TRUMP
Good job, Mike Pence.

                    PENCE
And what are you going to be doing, sir?

                                                   (CONTINUED)

                         TRUMP
I have to prepare for the G-Seven, Mike Pence. But first, I
have a very important meeting.

                         PENCE
I will leave you to it then, sir.

                              PENCE bows and exits as TRUMP
                              sits at the desk and reaches for
                              the phone.

                         TRUMP
                       (on phone)
Can you fetch my lawyer's checkbook?

                              Beat, and then the room goes
                              dark once more with another loud
                              bang.

                         ERIC (OFF)
Ouch.

ACT III, SCENE SEVEN | JUSTICE KENNEDY

                              A spotlight shines upon a BUS
                              STOP in the middle of the stage
                              where JUSTICE KENNEDY stands
                              waiting alone.

                         NARRATOR
                       (entering)
And so as for all new tasks are set, it falls to Putin to
ensure a way for a preferable Supreme Court quota soon to
be met. And so he follows for multiple days until comes the
chance to convince another to do as he says.

                              The NARRATOR exits as a man
                              wearing a hood enters and stands
                              behind KENNEDY.

                         PUTIN (UNDER HOOD)
Pst. Psssst. Hey.

                                             (CONTINUED)

CONTINUED:

                                     KENNEDY starts as he turns to
                                     see the man lowering his hood to
                                     reveal they are PUTIN.

                          KENNEDY
Oh. Vladimir. I didn't see you there.

                          PUTIN
I need have word with you.

                          KENNEDY
What do you mean have a word with me? I haven't done
anything wrong. I've done everything you've asked me to.

                          PUTIN
I need you resign seat on Supreme Court.

                          KENNEDY
Why would you want me to do that? I'm on your side

                          PUTIN
Because investigation continue and Donald likely to be
impeached soon. We have short time to secure court for
years that come.

                          KENNEDY
But I'm not that old. And I like my job.

                                       PUTIN pulls several photos from
                                     his pocket.

                          PUTIN
                      (showing first photo)
See this? This --

                          KENNEDY
That's me.

                          PUTIN
                    (showing second photo)
Good. Now, this. This be photo of man doing unspeakable
thing to warthog at local zoo.

                                             (CONTINUED)

                         KENNEDY
I don't get what you... Hold on, isn't that --

                         PUTIN
Yes, it be him. But we must not say, or he may sue.
                    (showing third photo)
This be activation key for well known photo editing
software package for P-C and other platform.

                    KENNEDY takes the photo.

                         PUTIN
We make multiple copy.

                         Beat.

                         KENNEDY
I'll resign my seat.

ACT III, SCENE EIGHT | THE G7 SUMMIT

                              The MANOIR RICHELIEU hotel in LA
                              MALBAIE, CANADA, where TRUMP
                              sits at a table at the back of
                              the stage while EMMANUEL MACRON
                              and ANGELA MERKEL stand to
                              confront him.

                         NARRATOR
                       (entering)
While for the President at home, the future looks to be
ever increasingly bleak, on the international stage, he
sees new opportunities and foreign policies ready for his
own unique Trump brand tweak.

                         MERKEL
                       (to TRUMP)
For the last time, Donald. Stop asking that man if you can
see the menu. He is the Prime Minister of Italy.

                                             (CONTINUED)

                         TRUMP
He was very rude to me, Angled Mackerel. I ordered a diet
cola from him over an hour ago, and he has still not
brought it to me.

                         NARRATOR
For leaving behind an investigation ongoing, it is to the
forty-fifth G-Seven summit in Quebec where he flies so he
can undertake some world leader elbowing.

                         MACRON
                    (to TRUMP)
He is not a waiter. And that woman who you asked security
to move along because she was sat on the floor crying, that
was Theresa May.

                         NARRATOR
For this is where gather the leader of the world's greatest
nations together all in one place, and their host for the
summit, a Prime Minister who many believe has the most
beautiful face.

                         JUSTIN TRUDEAU enters and shakes
                         hands with the NARRATOR.

                         TRUDEAU
Oh, hello. Welcome to Canada. Do you like my socks?
                    (showing off his socks)
You've got your very own pair in your hotel room. They come
with our compliments.

                         At the back of the stage, MERKEL
                         notices TRUDEAU.

                         MERKEL
                    (to MACRON)
Oh, Emmanuel, Justin is here.

                         MACRON turns around as TRUDEAU
                         approaches and shakes hands.

                         TRUDEAU
Welcome to Canada as our honored guests. It's good to see
you again, Chancellor Merkel. And you too President Macron.

                                              (CONTINUED)

                         TRUMP coughs loudly.

                         TRUDEAU
                        (to TRUMP)
Oh, I'm sorry. Would you like something for that cough
you've got there, Donald?

                         MACRON
                        (to TRUDEAU)
Thank you for the socks, Prime Minister. France thanks you
very much for your nation's kind generosity.

                         TRUDEAU
Oh, please. Call me Justin.

                         MERKEL
Can I call you Justin as well?

                         TRUMP coughs again.

                         TRUDEAU
                        (to TRUMP)
Are you certain I can't get you anything for that cough
there, Donald?

                         MACRON
                        (to TRUDEAU)
It really is a spectacular event that you are hosting for
us all here. I can only hope that we are able to live up to
the same next year.

                         TRUDEAU
Oh merci. Ce n'est vraiment rien du tout. Je suis sûr que
la France en fera plus qu'assez et j'ai hâte d'avoir
l'honneur d'être en votre présence lors de l'accueil de
l'année prochaine.

                         Beat.

                         MERKEL
                        (to herself)
Oh. He speaks French too.
                        (to TRUDEAU)
Can I have your autograph?

                                              (CONTINUED)

> TRUDEAU
> (laughing)

I don't do autographs. But how about we all get a photo
together?

> > > TRUDEAU walks over to the
> > > NARRATOR and hands them his
> > > phone.

> TRUDEAU

Do you mind?

> NARRATOR

Not at all.

> > > TRUDEAU leads MACRON and MERKEL
> > > to the center of the stage.

> TRUDEAU

Just here, I think.

> > > As they get into position, TRUMP
> > > stands, approaches from behind,
> > > and pushes his way to the front.

> TRUMP

America first.

> NARRATOR

And three... two... one...

> > > A flash fills the stage as
> > > MACRON, MERKEL, and TRUDEAU all
> > > pull faces behind TRUMP.

> > > TRUMP turns around as they start
> > > to laugh.

> TRUMP

What is so funny?

> MERKEL

Oh, nothing.

> > > > > (CONTINUED)

                              MACRON
Let's take another.

                    They get into position for a
                    second photo.

                              NARRATOR
Three... two... one...

                    Again, a flash as MACRON,
                    MERKEL, and TRUDEAU all pull
                    faces.

                              TRUDEAU
One more. For the memories

                              NARRATOR
Three... two... one...

                    Another flash as MACRON, MERKEL,
                    and TRUDEAU once more all pull
                    faces.

                              NARRATOR
I'm not sure I quite got it that time. I'll try again.
Three... two... one...

                    Another flash and MACRON,
                    MERKEL, and TRUDEAU pull faces
                    before MERKEL rushes forward
                    with her own phone.

                              MERKEL
Can you take one on my phone too?

                    The NARRATOR takes her phone as
                    MERKEL rushes back into place.

                              MERKEL
Oh, I do love my job sometimes.

                              TRUDEAU
Now, lunch, I think?

                                                    (CONTINUED)

                          MACRON
It would be an honor to dine with you, Prime Minister.

                              TRUDEAU gestures toward the
                              wings.

                          TRUDEAU
After you then, Mister President. Chancellor Merkel.

                              MACRON, MERKEL, and TRUDEAU go
                              to leave.

                          TRUMP
Where are you all going? I demand that you stay.
                    (noticing the NARRATOR)
Just you and me, huh?

                          NARRATOR
I'm contractually obliged to be here.

ACT III, SCENE NINE | TRUMP MEETS THE QUEEN

                              The NARRATOR remains on stage.

                          NARRATOR
And so was between Trudeau and Co the real discussions are
set to begin, a surprise is to await them for when they all
next awake from their hotel bed, for Donald J. Trump has
departed early to meet with a different world leader
instead.

Setting off on Air Force One to fly thousands of miles
across the sea, for that is where his next bilateral
meeting is set to be. With a dictator, a tyrant, that's the
term that some place, debatable, perhaps, but still it
rings true that their power comes solely through a family
trace.

This is why the President is so excited to greet a ruler
whom when many meet, they bow right down to her feet, and
with whom he seeks to get a photo to post with his tweet.
                          (MORE)

                                              (CONTINUED)
PERFORMANCE LICENSE EDITION   LICENSE # _ _ _ _ _ _ _ _

CONTINUED:
                         NARRATOR (CONT'D)
And so it's lucky for him that efforts have failed to have
him from the country banned, for it means that still he
gets his chance to meet the Queen of England.

                              The NARRATOR exits as lights go
                              up on a ROOM WITHIN BUCKINGHAM
                              PALACE, where PRINCE CHARLES and
                              PRINCE PHILIP sit halfway
                              through a game of chess.

                         CHARLES
Check.

                              PHILIP leans into the board.

                         PHILIP
I am checking.

                              THE QUEEN enters looking angry.

                         THE QUEEN
Whose bloody idea was it for me to meet with that orange
turd from our former colony?
                         (to CHARLES)
Charlie, is this your idea of a joke?

                         CHARLES
The Prime Minister called and asked if we could host him
for a day. I had to say yes, mummy. I did not know what
else I could have said.

                         THE QUEEN
You could have said that we were going out? We could still
say that we are going out, could we not?

                         CHARLES
Not really, mummy. They are due to arrive at any moment.

                         THE QUEEN
Any moment? Oh, bugger the biscuit corgis! I have not had
any time to lock away the crown jewels.

                              PHILIP makes a move on the
                              chessboard.

                                                  (CONTINUED)

CONTINUED:

                         PHILIP
                     (to CHARLES)
Check.

                         CHARLES
                     (to THE QUEEN)
It will all be okay, mummy. He is only here for one day.

                    CHARLES goes to make a move.

                         THE QUEEN
Charlie, if you dare that that queen, then I shall have you
sent to the Tower of London.

                         CHARLES

Oh. Well, I --

                         PHILIP
I think that is checkmate to me then, old boy. Bad luck
indeed.

                         THE QUEEN
                     (to CHARLES)
Bollock the scone swan! This is not going to be okay,
Charlie. You are not the one who will have to inform the
butler to clean up after him. I dare not think how long it
will take them to cover the scent.

                    CHARLES checks the board.

                         CHARLES
                     (to PHILIP)
Hold on, why do you have three kings?

                         PHILIP

I inherited them.

                         THE QUEEN
Chuff the afternoon finger sandwich! Will you stop playing
games? You are going to come with me right this moment and
help me greet him, Charlie.

                         CHARLES
Do I have to, mummy?

                                          (CONTINUED)

CONTINUED:

                         THE QUEEN
Who is Queen?

                         PHILIP
She has got you there.

                         THE QUEEN
I do not know why you are looking as though your fifty to
one came in at Ascott. You are coming too. You have much
more in common with him than I do.

                         PHILIP
Do I have to?

                         THE QUEEN
Who is Queen?

                         PHILIP
Bugger.

                         Lights fade on the scene as the
                         NARRATOR returns.

                         NARRATOR
Reluctant though all are to meet for the first time their
transatlantic head of state counterpart - a man whose name
in this country at least means simply a fart - they know
they have a diplomatic duty to fulfill, one that comes with
a rare opportunity for the most offensive in the room not
to be old Prince Phil.

                         The NARRATOR exits as the lights
                         go back up, this time on the
                         BUCKINGHAM PALACE VISITORS
                         ENTRANCE where a GUARD stands.

                         ERIC, dressed as a tourist,
                         enters and approaches the guard.

                         ERIC
Hey. You're wearing a hat. I want a hat.

                         ERIC reaches for the GUARD's
                         hat.

                                        (CONTINUED)

CONTINUED:

>   GUARD
> SIR, STAND BACK! DO NOT TOUCH THE QUEEN'S GUARD.

>   ERIC
>   (upset)
> I don't want a hat anymore.

>>   TRUMP enters with IVANKA and
>>   JUNIOR, the latter two also
>>   dressed as tourists.
>>
>>   JUNIOR rushes to ERIC.

>   JUNIOR
> Hey, buddy. What's up?

>   ERIC
>   (pointing at the GUARD)
> That man.

>>   JUNIOR confronts the GUARD.

>   JUNIOR
> Hey, bud, what do you think you're doing to my little
> brother?

>   GUARD
> **DO NOT QUESTION THE QUEEN'S GUARD.**

>>   TRUMP steps forward.

>   TRUMP
>   (to JUNIOR)
> Let me negotiate this, Donald Trump Junior.
>   (to the GUARD)
> Let us in.

>   GUARD
> **YOU WISH TO ENTER THE PALACE?**

>   TRUMP
> Yes.

(CONTINUED)

CONTINUED:

> GUARD
> (changed tone)

In which case, welcome to the official Buckingham Palace tour. Please note that all visitors and their bags will be required to undergo a security search. Do you have your tickets, please?

> TRUMP

I am here to see the Queen of not so Great Britain.

> GUARD

You are not permitted to visit the Queen as part of the tour, sir.

> TRUMP

Why not?

> GUARD

Because she is the Queen, sir.

> TRUMP

I was told that if I came here, then I would get to meet the Queen.

> GUARD

Sir, this is a tour. You get to see where the Queen lives, and you get a free pencil at the end, but you do not get to meet the Queen herself.

>> THE QUEEN enters with CHARLES
>> and PHILIP.

> THE QUEEN

Gob-smack the kerfuffled pork pie! That Fanta-colored flatulent fascist fornicator has already arrived.

> TRUMP
> (to the GUARD)

I hereby demand --

> GUARD

STEP BACK, SIR, OR I SHALL HAVE TO REMOVE YOU BY FORCE.

>> THE QUEEN approaches.

>>> (CONTINUED)

CONTINUED:

                    THE QUEEN
No. No. It is okay. He is the President of the United
States.

                    GUARD
I know who he is, your majesty. Why do you think I am
trying to remove him?

                    THE QUEEN
Very good point. But we do actually have to talk to him.
Even if he does look like a bloated pufferfish in need of
an enema.

                    GUARD
If that is your wish, your majesty.

                    THE QUEEN
No, of course, it is not my wish. Why would I wish for
this? And do not question your queen again, or I shall have
you arrest yourself for treason. Now, go away.

                    GUARD
Of course, your majesty.

                    The GUARD bows and exits.

                    THE QUEEN
So, you are Donald Trump, are you?

                    TRUMP
Listen, old lady, no autographs right now. I am waiting to
see some old bat in some hat.

                    ERIC
And I want a pencil.

                    THE QUEEN
I am the Queen.
                    (to CHARLES and PHILIP)
Charlie. Philip. Come over and greet our guests with me.

                    TRUMP pulls out a five-pound
                    note and holds it next to THE
                    QUEEN's head.

                                        (CONTINUED)

                    TRUMP
You do not look like the Queen.

                    THE QUEEN
No? What about if I turn this way?

                              THE QUEEN turns her head to
                              match the direction on the note.

                    TRUMP
According to this, you are only worth five English dollars.
Did you know that I am worth billions and billions of
dollars?

                    THE QUEEN
                    (ignoring TRUMP)
Shall I introduce you?
                    (gesturing at CHARLES)
This is my son, Charles, or Charlie as I call him. He is
the Prince of Wales.

                    CHARLES
So very lovely to meet you all.

                    TRUMP
Let me introduce you to my very great son... Eric Trump,
get out of the way.

                              TRUMP pulls JUNIOR in front of
                              ERIC.

                    TRUMP
This is Donald Trump Junior. He is just like me, only he is
junior.

                              JUNIOR reaches to shake hands
                              with them all, and then TRUMP.

                    JUNIOR
You know, it really is nice to meet all of you today.

                    TRUMP
It is very nice to meet you too, Donald Trump Junior. Let
me introduce you to the Queen.

                                        (CONTINUED)

                    THE QUEEN
Quite.
                    (gesturing at PHILIP)
And this is my husband and Charlie's father, the --

                    TRUMP
                    (to PHILIP)
You must be the king of the seas.

                    Beat.

                    THE QUEEN
No. He is the Duke of Edinburgh. Knacker the stewed trouser
press, are you always this dim?

                         PHILIP steps forward to shake
                         hands with TRUMP.

                    PHILIP
The wife was telling me that you are a keen racist. We must
talk about that. I am also a racist in my spare time, you
know?

                    TRUMP
That is fake news, Mister Edinburgh. I am not a racist.

                    PHILIP
That is fake news, Mister Edinburgh. I am not a racist.

                    TRUMP
I do not hate foreigners for no reason like a racist would.

                    PHILIP
Well then, why do you hate them?

                    TRUMP
I hate them because I can.

                    Beat.

                    PHILIP
You really are some offensive old fellow, are you not? You
must give me some tips on that before you depart.

                                                      (CONTINUED)

                         TRUMP brings IVANKA forward.

                         TRUMP
This is my daughter, Ivanka Trump.

                         IVANKA
You are all honored to meet me today.

                         THE QUEEN
                    (gesturing at ERIC)
And who is this young gentleman here?

                         TRUMP
That is Eric Trump. We have to bring him because...
                    (to JUNIOR)
Donald Trump Junior, why did we have to bring him?

                         JUNIOR
The babysitter canceled.

                         THE QUEEN
                    (to ERIC)
And tell me, young sir. Are you enjoying your visit to the
palace today?

                         ERIC
I saw a dog.

                         THE QUEEN
Well, gander at the antique fish pâte!

                         PHILIP
                    (to all)
That does remind me. I was in my study just the other
morrow reading the latest Bill O'Reilly when one of those
damned corgis came in and proceeded to take a massive dump
on the hearthrug. That is right, a massive ordure right in
front of me. And I had the fire on too. It did not half
cause the maid some trouble. The smell reminded me of that
time I had to visit Hull.

                         THE QUEEN
Philip.

                                             (CONTINUED)

CONTINUED:

                         PHILIP
Yes?

                         THE QUEEN
Do shut up.

                         PHILIP
Oh. Okay then.

                         THE QUEEN
                    (to CHARLES)
Charlie, why do not you take these three younger guests for
a tour of the palace?

                         CHARLES
I have an engagement in --

                         THE QUEEN
Do not make me cut your allowance again.

                         CHARLES
Yes, fine then.
                    (to JUNIOR, ERIC and IVANKA)
Do come this way.

                              CHARLES begins to lead ERIC,
                              IVANKA, and JUNIOR offstage.

                         CHARLES
So you are the President's children, are you?

                         ERIC
What kind of whale are you?

                         CHARLES
Sorry, what? I, oh...

                              CHARLES, ERIC, IVANKA, and
                              JUNIOR exit.

                         THE QUEEN
So, Mister Trump, I hear that you like to visit Scotland? I
have a place up there, do not you know?

                                             (CONTINUED)

TRUMP
Listen, Queenie. No one loves Scotland more than me, and
there is no one that Scotland loves more than Donald J.
Trump.

THE QUEEN
You will not get any disagreement from me. Why, do butter
the village bus stop! Half of them up there wish for me to
be abolished.

TRUMP
I have a golf course up there. Some say the best golf
course. I play golf. I play great. Do you play golf?

THE QUEEN
No. Not me personally. I have a man to do that for me.

TRUMP
You have a great place here.

THE QUEEN
Thank you very much. I inherited many of the objects you
can see.
                    (pointing at a painting)
Like this one here. My father was given it by Winston
Churchill himself.

PHILIP
It was told that Churchill used to have it hanging in his
office during the war.

THE QUEEN
                    (suddenly stern)
Anoint the palace cabbage patch! Philip, do not mention the
war.

PHILIP
Why not? He was on the same side as us.

THE QUEEN
No, he was not.

PHILIP
Oh, right.

                                                    (CONTINUED)

                         THE QUEEN
                        (to TRUMP)
Mister Trump, would you like to come and see the palace
gardens? I can show you around, and then we could get a
photographer to take some photographs for the newsprint?

                         TRUMP
Good idea, Queenie. And then after that, we should talk
business.

                              THE QUEEN begins to exit with
                              PHILIP following.

                         TRUMP
I have some great ideas to turn this place into a hotel.

                              TRUMP barges past THE QUEEN and
                              exits first. A moment later, he
                              returns.

                         TRUMP
Which way is it?

                         THE QUEEN
Right and then left.

                         TRUMP
Thank you.

                              TRUMP exits again.

                         THE QUEEN
Bloody hell and waltz with the gardener's budgerigar. He
really is as stupid as he looks on the television.

                              PHILIP and THE QUEEN exit as the
                              lights go down.

ACT III, SCENE TEN | PUTIN IN THE BATH

> As the NARRATOR enters a dark
> stage, from somewhere behind
> them comes the sound of bathroom
> singing.

NARRATOR

A meeting with royalty is one never to be forgotten, but
equally as necessary for the President is a need to fix at
home the issue of the public for on the truth they begin to
cotton. And so it is back in the air for a short few hours
across the sea, for a meeting that's to take place in a
third and neutral ground country.

But while the press gathers downstairs to ask questions in
their pre-scheduled conference, in his Helsinki hotel room
sits Trump's rendezvous bathing to remove his feelings so
tense.

> A light shines upon the scene
> behind the NARRATOR, where PUTIN
> sits in a bubble bath singing to
> himself. After a moment, he
> stops singing and looks around.

PUTIN

Can I not get just little privacy here?

> PUTIN shakes his head and then
> reaches for a bath brush to wash
> his back.

NARRATOR

But while Vladimir Putin sits to use his brush to scratch
his back, there is a clear sense that privacy is the
commodity which right now he does lack.

PUTIN

Of course. Anyone can see that. Here I wash, and hundreds
of people be watching.

> As the NARRATOR exits, there is
> a loud knock.

(CONTINUED)

CONTINUED:

> PUTIN
> (shouting out)
> What be it now? I am bathing.

>> There is another knock.

> PUTIN
> Fine. Come on in. But be quick.

>> DMITRY and PETROV enter with the
>> latter carrying a soccer ball.

> DMITRY
> Comrade Putin, sir.

> PUTIN
> You know, most world leaders be able to wash without
> disturbance. What do you want?

> PETROV
> Our apologies, Comrade, sir. We do not mean to disturb, but
> we bring news.

> PUTIN
> What news?

>> PETROV holds the ball out.

> PETROV
> Ball.

>> Beat.

> PUTIN
> I be missing something.

> DMITRY
> We fit camera and microphone as instructed, Comrade.

> PUTIN
> You came whole way here and disturb bath just so you be
> able to tell me you put camera in ball?

>> (CONTINUED)

CONTINUED:

                    PETROV

And microphone, Comrade.

                    PUTIN

Could news not wait until after I bathe?

                    DMITRY

We thought you enjoy news right away, Comrade.

                    PUTIN

You two really be largest idiots in whole of Russia. If you
be American, you be in Senate by now.

                    PETROV

Comrade, if I can ask, why you need ball?

                    DMITRY

Did you not have idea to give Comrade Trump rubber duck for
same purpose?

                    PUTIN

Donald keep rubber duck in bathroom, and it not be sight
anyone should ever see.

                    DMITRY

I see.

                    PUTIN

No. You really do not want. That man fake tans in way not
fit for human audience.

                    PETROV

Is there anything else you need, Comrade?

                    PUTIN

Yes. I need you leave Putin to bathe. I have hair of mine
to wash.

                    DMITRY

But, Comrade, you do not --

                    PUTIN

Leave.

                                        (CONTINUED)

>   DMITRY and PETROV exit as PUTIN
>   begins to sing once more.
>
>   The lights fade.

ACT III, SCENE ELEVEN | HELSINKI

>   Lights up on two podiums set out
>   in front of the flags of the
>   United States and Russia. In
>   front of the podiums sits the
>   ENSEMBLE (as PRESS, excluding
>   PRESS #2).

                              NARRATOR
                            (entering)
Ready to stand and share confident the United States aims,
all while unabashedly furthering his string of provably
false claims, Donald Trump is the first to arrive, ready to
with Putin publicly beg, steal, and foremost contrive.

>   TRUMP enters at the edge of the
>   stage and stands typing on his
>   phone.

                              NARRATOR
While now fully relaxed and ready for any question that may
lie ahead, Vladimir Putin is just moments behind, though
having forgotten what still sits atop his head.

>   The NARRATOR exits as PUTIN
>   enters by TRUMP wearing a
>   flowery shower cap.

                              PUTIN
Donald. I be glad to have talk before press.

                              TRUMP
Hold on. I am just sending a tweet.
                            (to himself, reading)
"And the Queen was very mean to me. Sad. Very bad for her
people." And send.

                                              (CONTINUED)

CONTINUED:

                              TRUMP puts his phone away.

                              TRUMP
What is it, Comrade Vladimir Putin, sir?

                              PUTIN
I be worried members of your press ask question they should
not ask. Awkward question.

                              TRUMP
I do not understand.

                              PUTIN
About Russia. They ask about Russia. They think Russia had
hand in election win of yours.

                              TRUMP
But you did?

                              PUTIN
Actually, we had two hand, Donald. But point be they should
not know. You need tell them that Russia did not have
involvement in election.

                              TRUMP
Can you not deal with them?

                              PUTIN
There be laws against Russian approach in Finland.

                              TRUMP
So what do I do?

                              PUTIN
I just say. Tell them Russia had no part.

                              TRUMP
I understand.

                              PUTIN
Tell them you be sure of this.

                              TRUMP
I understand.

                                                          (CONTINUED)

> PUTIN
Good. Now let us go out there.

                    PUTIN sets off toward the
                    podiums.

> TRUMP
I do not understand.

                    PUTIN stops and turns back.

> TRUMP
Why are you wearing a hat?

> PUTIN
I be wearing nothing on head.

> TRUMP
I can see it.

> PUTIN
I wear nothing on head, Donald.
                    (beat)
Now come. And just do what I do.

                    PUTIN and TRUMP make their way
                    to their podiums.

> PUTIN
                    (to PRESS)
Stand.
                    (beat)
No, really. When I enter room, you stand. Now. Stand. All
of you.

                    The PRESS stand.

> PUTIN
Good. Now sit.

                    The PRESS sit.

> PUTIN
Members of press, welcome.

                                        (CONTINUED)

                                        PUTIN puts his arm out as though
                                        to greet them. TRUMP copies him.

                         PUTIN
Welcome to Helsinki.

                         TRUMP
Welcome to Helsinki.

                         PUTIN
I be glad to have opportunity to speak with Donald today to
discuss ties between nation. And we be glad now to answer
question you have.

                         TRUMP
I am glad to have the opportunity to speak with Donald
Trump today to discuss the ties between our nations. And we
are glad to have this chance to answer any questions you
have.

                                        PUTIN coughs. TRUMP copies him.

                         PUTIN
Donald. What are you doing?

                         TRUMP
Donald Trump. What are you doing?

                         PUTIN
DONALD!

                         TRUMP
You told me to do what you do.

                         PUTIN
Not everything I do.

                                        PUTIN scratches an itch. TRUMP
                                        copies him.

                         PUTIN
Just... Do not be weird.
                    (to PRESS)
Okay. Who has question?

                                                      (CONTINUED)

CONTINUED:

                              The PRESS remains silent as
                              TRUMP pulls his phone back out.

                    PUTIN
No question at all? Not one?

                    The PRESS remain silent.

                    PUTIN
There be major news in your country about belief that
Russia hacked election and not one of you have question?

                    PRESS #1
We don't need to ask them. We already know you'll deny it,
and we already know what the President has to say

                    PUTIN
How could it be you know what Donald is to say? He answer
no question.

                    PRESS #6
                    (holding up their phone)
He tweeted.
                    (reading from phone)
"Just spoken to Vlad. Good meeting. He tells me that I must
tell you all Russia had no involvement in the election.
Dot. Dot. Dot" --

                    TRUMP
                    (to himself, reading)
"Dot. Dot. Dot. And now I have to have press conference
with loser press. Total losers. Very sad." And tweet.

                    PUTIN
DONALD!

                    TRUMP looks up.

                    TRUMP
I was tweeting.

                    PUTIN
                    (to PRESS)
Okay. Is there any question?

                                        (CONTINUED)

>   PRESS #3
Yes. Hello. Washington Post here. What exactly are you
wearing on your head?

>   PUTIN
They be daffodils. I like way they look.
>   (to PRESS)
Next question.

>   PRESS #4
N-B-C here.

>   PUTIN
Go ahead.

>   PRESS #4
Yes. You've just mentioned how there is a belief in America
by many that Russia interfered in the two thousand and
sixteen elections, and recently there have also been
several alleged Russian spies that have been arrested --

>   PUTIN
Arrested? I know not of arrest.
>   (to TRUMP)
Donald. Do you know of arrest?

>   TRUMP
I do not know anything, Vladimir Putin, almighty. N-B-C is
just talking fake news.

>   PRESS #4
But, Mister President, you tweeted about them just an hour
ago.

>   TRUMP
>   (drawn out)
Fake news.

>   PUTIN
Continue with question.

>   (CONTINUED)

                         PRESS #4
Do you think that these beliefs of Russian interference and
these arrests are going to damage relations between the
United States and Russia?

                         PUTIN laughs.

                         PUTIN
Damage relation? No. There be no damage relation. Relation
between Putin's Russia and Putin's America be at all-time
high.

                                   PUTIN gestures to someone in the
                                   wings.

                         PUTIN
You actually remind me I have gift for Donald to show good
friends we are.

                                   PETROV enters carrying the
                                   soccer ball and hands it to
                                   PUTIN.

                         PUTIN
This be ball from World Cup Russia set to win this year.

                                   PUTIN hands the ball to TRUMP as
                                   PETROV exits.

                         PUTIN
Donald. I wish you take ball as token of good thing.

                         TRUMP
Thank you, Vladimir Putin. I will treasure this.

          TRUMP   PUTIN
I have a special shelf in my   Just please do not keep in
bathroom.   bathroom.

                         PUTIN
No. God. Please. Anywhere but that.
                    (to PRESS)
Any more question?

                                                    (CONTINUED)

                          PRESS #5
Fox News here. I have a question for President Trump.

                           TRUMP
Go ahead, Fox News.

                          PRESS #5
I want to ask you about the Supreme Court.

                           PUTIN
Finally. Good question.

                          PRESS #5
President Trump, the resignation of Justice Kennedy from
the Supreme Court has left a vacancy for you to fill. Have
you got any ideas of who you might nominate yet?

                           TRUMP
That is a great question, and I have a great answer. I am
going to nominate someone who is great. I cannot tell you
who yet, but they will be great.

                          PRESS #5
Can you not give us any name?

                           TRUMP
                         (to PUTIN)
Vladimir Putin, who am I going to --

                           PUTIN
Donald! Be quiet.
                         (to PRESS)
Next question. No more question? Good. Leave.

                          PRESS #1
I have a question.

                           PUTIN
No. No more question. You go now. Go before Putin annex
Helsinki and have you arrested.

                          PRESS #1
But --

                                              (CONTINUED)

CONTINUED:

                         PUTIN
GO!

                    The PRESS leaves in a hurry.

                         TRUMP
                        (to PUTIN)
Was it something I said?

                         PUTIN
Donald. You do not ask me suspicious question when there be
witness.

                         TRUMP
But who am I going to nominate?

                         PUTIN
Putin not know. I thought, perhaps you choose. Can you
think of anyone who be good?

                         TRUMP
Ivanka?

                         PUTIN
No. Not Ivanka. They need have experience. Why not you go
back home and think about people?

                         TRUMP
Wait. I have an idea.

                         PUTIN
Who?

                         TRUMP
It has gone.

                         PUTIN
Look. Donald. Just choose someone who be not... bad.

                    Lights out.

ACT III, SCENE TWELVE | BRETT KAVANAUGH

>   The NARRATOR enters.

NARRATOR
While all across America suspicious as to Russia's election involvement continue to rise, Donald Trump returns home to implement a way to ensure his stability, a new seat on the Supreme Court, his pick for the nation still a surprise. For who to choose is the question that on his mind is a plague, for he needs naught but a man to save him a trip to The Netherland's The Hague. But eventually, a name comes to him, and so he sets off to the bar, for he has a new job to hire onto his team, Brett Kavanaugh.

>   The NARRATOR exits as the lights
>   go up on a BAR is D.C., Where a
>   JUDGE sits relaxed at the bar
>   talking to the BARTENDER.

JUDGE
And so the teacher asked my son what comes at the end of a sentence and he answered an appeal.

>   The BARTENDER laughs.

BARTENDER
Can I get you another, judge?

>   The JUDGE finishes his drink.

JUDGE
Yeah. I've got time for one more.

>   TRUMP enters and looks around.

JUDGE
Did I ever tell you about the Christmas card I got from a lawyer last year? He said he wishes, but cannot guarantee, my family a happy Christmas.

>   The BARTENDER laughs again as
>   TRUMP approaches.

>   (CONTINUED)

CONTINUED:

                    TRUMP
I am looking for a judge.

                  BARTENDER
            (gesturing at the JUDGE)
Well, here's a Judge right here.

                    TRUMP
              (to the JUDGE)
Brett Kavanaugh, I am here to --

                    JUDGE
I'm not Brett Kavanaugh.

                    TRUMP
Do you know Brett Kavanaugh?

                              At the far end of the stage,
                              BRETT KAVANAUGH enters and
                              stands watching.

                    JUDGE
          (gesturing at the BARTENDER)
He does.

                  BARTENDER
Yeah. I know Brett Kavanaugh, alright.

                    TRUMP
Do you know where I can find him?

                  BARTENDER
Do I know where you can find Brett Kavanaugh?
                  (beat)
Sure. I know where you can find Brett Kavanaugh.

                              A pause, and then the BARTENDER
                              points over to KAVANAUGH.

                  BARTENDER
He's over there.

                              As attention turns to KAVANAUGH,
                              he takes a long sniff.

                                    (CONTINUED)

                          KAVANAUGH
ARE WE READY TO DO SOME BOOFING?

                                        Loud music begins to play as
                                        KAVANAUGH puts his hands in the
                                        air. A moment later, the
                                        BARTENDER kicks something behind
                                        the bar, and silence falls.

                          BARTENDER
Shut that stuff up, Brett. There's a guy here to see you.

                          KAVANAUGH approaches.

                          KAVANAUGH
                          (to TRUMP)
I didn't expect to ever see you here, Mister President. I
didn't think that you were cool. I thought you were a
lightweight.
                          (to the BARTENDER)
I'm meeting P-J and Squee here in ten, so I'll take three
beers.

                          BARTENDER
Three beers coming up.

                          KAVANAUGH
And they'll take one each as well.

                          BARTENDER
Five beers coming up.

                          KAVANAUGH
                          (to TRUMP)
I like beer, Mister President. Do you like beer?

                                        The BARTENDER places a beer on
                                        top of the bar. KAVANAUGH takes
                                        it and downs it in one.

                          KAVANAUGH
                          (while drinking)
DOWN! DOWN! DOWN! DOWN! DOWN! DOWN! DOWN! DOWN! DOWN!

                                                      (CONTINUED)

CONTINUED:

                        KAVANAUGH slams the glass back
                        onto the bar.

                  KAVANAUGH

I love beer. You know how you love golden showers? Well, I
love them too. Mine are beer.

                        KAVANAUGH takes another long
                        sniff.

                  KAVANAUGH

Have you ever played devil's triangle, Mister President? I
can show you how to play if you want?

                  TRUMP

Brett Kavanaugh, are you drunk?

                        KAVANAUGH bends and looks back
                        through his own legs.

                  KAVANAUGH

No. I don't think so. I can still feel my feet.

                        KAVANAUGH stands back up.

                  KAVANAUGH

So what brings you here?

                  TRUMP

I came to ask if you would like to join the Supreme Court.

                  KAVANAUGH

The Supreme Court? Sounds cool. What would I have to do?

                  TRUMP

Dress up as a wizard and make sure I don't get arrested.

                  KAVANAUGH

I'm not sure. I have a pretty full schedule. When would you
need me?

                  TRUMP

For the rest of your life.

                              (CONTINUED)

CONTINUED:

                    KAVANAUGH
Hold on. I'll check my calendar.

                              KAVANAUGH pulls a large folded
                              calendar from his pocket,
                              flattens it, and then begins to
                              examine it.

                    KAVANAUGH
I'll have to move a few lifting sessions around, but I can
make it work.

                              The BARTENDER down a second beer
                              and KAVANAUGH downs it.

                    KAVANAUGH
So when do I start?

                    TRUMP
You have to be confirmed by loser Congress first.

                    KAVANAUGH
That bunch of asses? Easy. Now can I get you a beer, Mister
President?
                    (to the BARTENDER)
Two more beers.
                    (to TRUMP)
And what do you want?

                    TRUMP
I am going to leave now. Even for me, you are too much.

                              TRUMP goes to leave.

                    KAVANAUGH
                    (calling after TRUMP)
Hey, Mister President.

                              TRUMP turns back as KAVANAUGH
                              downs the third beer from the
                              BARTENDER.

                    KAVANAUGH
Does it matter if I don't have a great past?

                                             (CONTINUED)

>   Beat.

                         TRUMP
Apparently not.

ACT III, SCENE THIRTEEN | THE KAVANAUGH HEARING

>   On stage, a SENATE COMMITTEE
>   ROOM set out for a hearing. Next
>   to it, a SMALL LOCKER ROOM where
>   KAVANAUGH sits on the floor
>   doing sit-ups with a towel.

                         NARRATOR
                         (entering)
And so now chosen is the President's second Supreme Court
pick. Though his chosen one's confirmation is set to be
anything but slick. For questions soon arise about Brett
Kavanaugh's past, and before long, a collection of claims
has quickly amassed. And so in the Senate, a committee
hearing is held, an opportunity hope Republicans, to ensure
that all uncertainties are quelled.

>   The NARRATOR exits as Senators
>   JOHN CORNYN, TED CRUZ, JEFF
>   FLAKE, LINDSEY GRAHAM, CHUCK
>   GRASSLEY, and ORRIN HATCH enter.

                         GRASSLEY
Okay. Now let's take our seats and get this over with
before the Democrats get back from lunch.

>   The group take their seats.

                         GRASSLEY
Earlier, we heard from a woman. That was interesting. She
said some things and I'm sure that some of us listened. But
now, we are going to come to the main event and talk to the
legend that is Judge Brett Kavanaugh.

                         HATCH
Are we not waiting for that woman we hired to do our jobs
for us?

>   (CONTINUED)

                          CORNYN
The political prop we hired to look as though we care?

                          HATCH
That's the one.

                          GRASSLEY
I really don't think we need a woman this time around. I'm
sure that we can question this, I think we can all agree,
cool dude, on our own.

                                    There is a murmur of agreement
                                    from all except FLAKE, who
                                    audibly gulps.

                          GRASSLEY
Okay. So if we're all ready --

                                    The sudden appearance of DIANE
                                    FEINSTEIN from under the desk
                                    interrupts proceedings.

                          FEINSTEIN
Now hold on one moment.

                          GRASSLEY
Ranking Member Feinstein. What are you doing hiding under
the desk?

                          FEINSTEIN
I was eating my lunch down here because I had a feeling
that you bastards would try something clever.

                          GRASSLEY
I don't know what --

                          FEINSTEIN
And then I remembered that you're all Republicans so it
wouldn't be clever. It would just be evil.

                          GRASSLEY
Well, we're just about to begin.

                                                        (CONTINUED)

FEINSTEIN
Are we not waiting for the rest of my party.

GRASSLEY
We really don't have the time, I'm afraid. I have to go for
a round of golf later on, and Lindsey Graham here, he has
his first anger management session tonight.

GRAHAM
**IT'S BECAUSE I GET REAL ANGRY NOW. I'M ANGRY THAT THE WHITE
MAN IS UNDER ATTACK. I'M ANGRY THAT --**

                    GRASSLEY bangs a gavel.

GRAHAM
I yield my time.

GRASSLEY
Okay, so now I think it's time that we brought in he who is
the man, the one and the only, Brett Kavanaugh.

                    KAVANAUGH stands, wipes his face
                    with the towel, flexes, and then
                    approaches the SENATORS.

GRAHAM
**AND IN THE RED CORNER, INTRODUCING JUDGE BRETT KAVANAUGH. A
FORMER INTER-STATE BOOFING CHAMPION IN HIGH SCHOOL, HE WAS
THE FIRST MAN TO DISCOVER ALL FOUR CORNERS OF THE DEVIL'S
TRIANGLE, AND HE IS YOUR NEXT JUSTICE OF THE SUPREME COURT!**

                    KAVANAUGH takes his seat, and as
                    silence falls, he sniffs.

KAVANAUGH
**Before any of you ask me a question, I have a question for
all of you.**

GRASSLEY
Ask away, Mister Kavanaugh.

KAVANAUGH
Do any of you have a beer?

                                              (CONTINUED)

CONTINUED:

>   GRASSLEY looks around at his
>   fellow SENATORS as all, except
>   FEINSTEIN, who looks disgusted,
>   shake their heads.

                    GRASSLEY
I'm afraid not.

                    KAVANAUGH
Dang it. Not even a light? I'm feeling real parched right
about now.

                    GRASSLEY
We can offer you a glass of water?

                    KAVANAUGH
I'll take a pint of that.

                    GRASSLEY
Okay. Well, while we wait for that, would you like to give
us your opening statement, Judge Kavanaugh?

                    KAVANAUGH
I'll do that. I just... I need a moment.

>   Overcome with emotion, KAVANAUGH
>   sniffs and wipes his face before
>   pulling a piece of paper from
>   his pocket.

                    KAVANAUGH
I'm sorry. It's just a hard time for me right now. And
these words, they are my words. They come from deep within
my heart. I sat down, on my own one night, and I came up
with these words which I offer to you now.
                    (beat, then reading from the
                     paper)
"You should begin by telling them that you're grateful for
the opportunity to clear your name, Brett. That will get
them onto your side right from the start."
                    (looking up),
I am grateful for the opportunity to clear my name --

                                              (CONTINUED)

FEINSTEIN
I'd like to say something.

GRASSLEY bangs a gavel.

GRASSLEY
Continue, Brett Kavanaugh.

KAVANAUGH
(reading)
"After that, tell them that you're --"

The NARRATOR enters with a
bottle of water.

KAVANAUGH
WHAT? I asked for a pint of water. Not some dumb plastic
bottle. Do I look like some kid who can't use a big boy
glass?

NARRATOR
There weren't any glasses.

KAVANAUGH takes the bottle and
fails in his attempt to open it.

KAVANAUGH
CAN YOU... Can you open it for me?

The NARRATOR takes the bottle,
opens it with ease, and then
hands it back to KAVANAUGH.

KAVANAUGH
Thank you.

KAVANAUGH takes one mouthful
from the bottle and then empties
the rest over his face before
throwing the bottle to one side
and returning to his notes.

(CONTINUED)

CONTINUED:

                          KAVANAUGH
                          (reading)
"Don't forget to tell them that you're incest..."
                        (to the NARRATOR)
What does this say?

                          NARRATOR
                        (leaning in)
Innocent.

                          The NARRATOR exits.

                          KAVANAUGH
                        (reading)
"Don't forget to tell them that you're innocent."
                    (looking up, angry)
Innocent. I'm innocent, I tell you.

                          GRASSLEY
Well, it has me convinced.

                          CRUZ
Chair, if I could suggest? I don't think we need to hear
anything else here today.

                          GRASSLEY
I quite --

                          FEINSTEIN
No. I've got questions.

                          KAVANAUGH
WHAT? How can you have questions? The word of my people has
been good for centuries. How can you not believe me? For
centuries, I'm telling you.

                          GRASSLEY
Judge Kavanaugh does have a point.

                          FEINSTEIN
I've got questions.

                                 (CONTINUED)

                         GRASSLEY
Okay then. Ranking Member Feinstein, what are your
questions.

                         FEINSTEIN
Thank you.
                     (to KAVANAUGH)
Mister Kavanaugh, today we have heard first-hand testimony,
and over the past few weeks, we have heard of many accounts
by other strong women, all of which corroborate. If you
really are as innocent as you claim, why aren't you
agreeing to a formal investigation?

                         KAVANAUGH
I want an investigation. I called for an investigation.

                         FEINSTEIN
So you are asking for a formal F-B-I investigation?

                         KAVANAUGH
We don't need an investigation. Why would we need an
investigation?

                         FEINSTEIN
You don't want to prove that you're innocent?

                         KAVANAUGH
I have already proven that I'm innocent. Have you not seen
my calendars?

                         FEINSTEIN
I was just about to get to those.

                              FEINSTEIN holds up a collection
                              of calendars featuring beach
                              models.

                         FEINSTEIN
Mister Kavanaugh, are these your calendars?

                         KAVANAUGH
If they have extreme ironing every Tuesday at eight with
Squee, then yes.

                                              (CONTINUED)

CONTINUED:

> FEINSTEIN
> Okay, so my first question is why have you stuck our face
> over the faces of all of these male models?

> KAVANAUGH
> Duh. It's what we all used to do.

> FEINSTEIN
> My second question is whose face have you stuck over the
> female models?

> KAVANAUGH
> That's Squee. Yeah, me and P-J thought he looks funny with
> boobs.

> FEINSTEIN
> Mister Kavanaugh, what sort of person keeps all of their
> calendars from their youth just in case hey may need them
> to try to prove they never sexually assaulted anyone --

> KAVANAUGH
> I --

> FEINSTEIN
> Hold on. I have a follow-up. What sort of person does that?
> And why would you want to admit to being that person?

> Beat.

> KAVANAUGH
> Are you drunk?

> FEINSTEIN
> If I wasn't at the start I will need to be by the end. Can
> we return to my question?

>> GRAHAM begins to bang his fist
>> on the desk in protest.

> GRAHAM
> Chair, I must object to this line of questioning. It is
> inappropriate at best and discrimination at its worst.

(CONTINUED)

                         FEINSTEIN
I'd still like an answer.

                    GRASSLEY bangs a gavel.

                         GRASSLEY
Lindsey Graham has the floor.

                         GRAHAM
Thank you, Mister Chairman. You know, this whole situation
here reminds me of a documentary I once watched on the
great Fox network.

It was a piece that told the story of a hardworking and
self-made white man who had made many sacrifices to get
where he was. And you know, people hated him for it. They
hated that a white man could still be successful in
America.

But let me tell you, this is America and he was still
successful. And when opportunity came, he took it and he
drilled for that oil to keep it in the hands of the
hardworking and deserving white American patriot.

But the people, they got real angry about it. They were
mad. And what did they do? I'll tell you what they did do.
They shot him. But no one could work out who had shot him
because every last person hated this white man's guts.

He was persecuted, just like Judge Brett Kavanaugh here. In
the end, it turned out that a baby had shot him. That's
right, a baby. And that is why we need --

                         FEINSTEIN
Senator Graham, are you talking about the Simpson's episode
where someone shot Mister Burns?

                         Beat.

                         GRAHAM
I want it on the record that it was a convincing portrayal
from all involved.

                                              (CONTINUED)

CONTINUED:

                         FEINSTEIN
Nineteen ninety-five called, they want their cultural
references back.

                    GRASSLEY bangs a gavel.

                         GRAHAM
I Yield my time.

                         GRASSLEY
Senator Flake. You've been quiet so far.

                         FLAKE
I'm just sitting here watching and thinking that this has
got to be a turning point. This is not a time for us to be
putting party over country. I've looked at all the
evidence, and I've listened to comments from my
constituents who have genuine concerns about this man here.

I'm also in a unique position, stepping down in just a few
months, so I don't need to worry about how my decision
plays with the Republican base. All things considered, I
think that the only right thing to do is not to vote in
favor.

                         FEINSTEIN
I always knew that you had a heart --

                         FLAKE
And that is why I will be voting to confirm Judge Brett
Kavanaugh.

                         FEINSTEIN
You're a real asshole, Jeff.

                    GRASSLEY bangs a gavel.

                         FLAKE
I yield my opinions.

                         GRASSLEY
I think that brings us nicely to voting. Senator Cornyn?

                                                    (CONTINUED)

CONTINUED:

                              CORNYN
Aye.

                              GRASSLEY
Senator Cruz?

                              CRUZ
Aye.

                              GRASSLEY
Senator Feinstein?

                              FEINSTEIN
No. Obviously.

                              GRASSLEY
Senator Flake?

                              FLAKE
Aye.

                              GRASSLEY
Senator Graham?

                              GRAHAM
Let me tell you right now, Chair. This is an honor for me
to vote for this man. Aye, it is. Aye is most definitely
is.

                              GRASSLEY
Senator Hatch?

                              HATCH
Aye.

                              GRASSLEY
And finally, Judge Kavanaugh?

                              KAVANAUGH
I vote in favor.

                              FEINSTEIN
Wait a minute, why does he get a vote?

                                                  (CONTINUED)

>   GRASSLEY bangs a gavel.

                    GRASSLEY
Judge Brett Kavanaugh, I think you're going to be our next
Justice of the Supreme Court.

ACT III, SCENE FOURTEEN | FLAKE & COLLINS

>   On stage, a single ELEVATOR
>   sands in a CAPITOL CORRIDOR.

                    NARRATOR
                    (entering)
And so to the Senate moves Kavanaugh's confirmation, not
least due to Jeff Flake's sudden spinal ablation. But from
no Republican comes the hope of any salvation, for not one
of them finds all that they are learning the least bit
concerning to be towards the nomination anything but
discerning. But the reality is that when it comes time for
all to vote, the people outside are sat taking note. And
for no one elected, is there a place left to hide, not now
their political careers have all but died.

>   As the NARRATOR exits, FLAKE
>   enters and goes to call the
>   elevator.
>
>   The elevator doors open, and
>   FLAKE steps inside as SUSAN
>   COLLINS enters after him.

                    COLLINS
Can you hold it for me?

>   As the doors begin to close,
>   FLAKE pushes a button, and they
>   reopen for COLLINS to join him.

                    COLLINS
Good afternoon, Jeff. We really got them all today, didn't
we? For a moment, they actually believed that we were going
to do the right thing and vote against Kavanaugh.

                                        (CONTINUED)

CONTINUED:

> As the doors begin to close once
> more, voices of protest come
> from offstage, and FLAKE holds
> them open.

                    FLAKE
You know, Susan. I think I'm going to take the stairs.

                    COLLINS
I think I'll join you.

> COLLINS and FLAKE exit together
> as the lights fade out.

                    COLLINS (OFF)
I'm going to write a letter to someone about this. I really
disapprove of voters having their own opinions.

<u>END OF ACT III</u>

                                                (CONTINUED)

ACT IV : "THE THIRD YEAR"

ACT IV, SCENE ONE | OBAMA IN TAHITI

> With the audience seated for the
> final act, the auditorium falls
> dark and silent as the gentle
> sound of crashing waves and
> tropical music grows in volume.

NARRATOR
(entering)
With the half-way point of the Trump presidency now fast
approaching, soon to come are the Midterms where Democrats
hope to capitalize by undertaking Republican seat poaching.
All the while, the situation for Donald himself becomes
ever more serious, and his ability to try to stand tall
above it all ever more increasingly less imperious.

For on each every side come new allegations and
investigations that raise questions he fights hard to duck,
not so stressful though is the life of his predecessor. For
his life is calm on a South Pacific island where he lies
back to enjoy the sun not having to give a fu --

> A loud beep interrupts.

NARRATOR
(shouting out)
Oh, come on! There are four acts to this show. Can't I just
say it once?

> The NARRATOR exits as lights go
> up on a BEACHFRONT RESTAURANT
> where a table stands waiting.
>
> ANDERSON COOPER and BARACK OBAMA
> enter, both dressed for warm
> weather.

OBAMA
(gesturing at the table)
You know, Anderson...
(MORE)

(CONTINUED)

CONTINUED:
                          OBAMA (CONT'D)
I would say take this seat here, but... they belong to the
establishment that we have chosen to feast in this
afternoon... You could always borrow it... but it is not
mine to permit you leave of for any period of time.

                         COOPER and OBAMA take their
                         seats and pick up menus.

                            OBAMA
If I could make a small request?... Please refrain from
communicating with those at Fox News that I am borrowing
this chair here... For eight years, they never really
forgave me for temporarily acquiring with the intention of
later returning to the owner... anything at all.

                         COOPER looks across the stage as
                         though to address a camera.

                            COOPER
                       (to the "camera")
Welcome to this special edition of Anderson Cooper Three
Sixty. Today, I am on the beautiful island of Tahiti in
French Polynesia to meet with former President, Barack
Obama, to bring you an exclusive interview live... at the
time of recording, which we will later edit and broadcast
to you, our viewers, not live.

                         OBAMA attempts to look in the
                         same direction.

                            OBAMA
Anderson... with whom is it that you are trying to solicit
a consultation with?... There is no one in that location.

                         A WAITER enters and approaches
                         their table.

                            WAITER
Good evening. I will be your waiter for your meal.

                            OBAMA
Waiter?

                                              (CONTINUED)

PERFORMANCE LICENSE EDITION   LICENSE # _ _ _ _ _ _ _

                          WAITER
That is correct, your waiter.

                          OBAMA
                     (pointing)
But what if we want to wait... over in that nearby locality
instead?
                     (beat, then to COOPER)
It really is a great dining facility here, Anderson... You
know, I was in here just a couple of moons back, and I saw
five people walk into the bar... In just as many sixty-
second increments... of time... The sixth person was much
luckier as they remembered... to duck.

                          COOPER
We sure are missing that sense of humor, Mister President.

                          WAITER
Can I take your orders?

                          OBAMA
Will we get them back again later on?

                          COOPER
                     (to the WAITER)
I'll take the steak.

                          OBAMA
And I will also take the tenderloin... of a cow or a bull.
But make my own lean... and by that, I mean that I want the
chef to cook it... while stood on just one of their lower
limbs.

                          WAITER
                     (to COOPER)
And would you like the soup or the salad to start?

                          COOPER
I'll take the salad.

                          WAITER
                     (to OBAMA)
And for you, sir? Would you like the soup or the salad?

                                              (CONTINUED)

                              OBAMA
Super salad?... I will be okay with the regular, standard,
ordinary selection... of prepared greeneries and selected
vegetables... thank you.

                    The WAITER exits.

                              COOPER
So, Mister President, how have things been?

                              OBAMA
Well... there have been some tenacious winds causing quite
a number of disheveled asperous crests out on the aqua on
some days... but most of the time... the circumstances
surrounding the briny deep... are more than ideal for some
surfing... and if the temperament is most agreeable... even
some paragliding also.

                              COOPER
And have you been keeping up with everything that's been
going on around the world? Do you have any concerns about
the recent developments with the situation in North Korea?

                              OBAMA
North Korea?... Not my problem... That nation is no longer
a complication, nor a dilemma... that gives me a headache
anymore... Fuck them.

                    The NARRATOR returns.

                              NARRATOR
                         (shouting out)
He's allowed one.
                         (beat)
Yes. I know who he is.

                              OBAMA
Narrator... could you please acquire on my behalf the wine
list?... And by that, I don't infer a printout... of Donald
Trump's ante meridiem Twitter feed.

                    The NARRATOR exits.

                                             (CONTINUED)

COOPER
Is there anything that concerns you anymore?

OBAMA
Well, now I have glanced over the news and noted a couple
of cases... in Wisconsin, the elected chamber there were
attempting to pass a law... to make spherical hay bails
illegal... It was something about cattle not getting... a
four-sided square meal... And then was also a story of a
kidnapping... over in a school in Massachusetts.

COOPER
I don't remember reading about that.

OBAMA
You wouldn't have heard... It ended quite amicably... The
kid awoke from his slumber before the teacher... observed
that he was sleeping.

                         The WAITER returns with their
                         starters, which they place on
                         the table.

WAITER
Please accept my apologies for your wait.

OBAMA
Weight?... Hey, are you calling Obama fat?
                    (beat)
I'm just jesting with you.

                         The WAITER exits.

COOPER
It looks like they do a good salad at this place.

OBAMA
You should wait for the steaks... The steaks rank very
highly... The chef who prepares them for our consumption
does not get paid... if they are not very good.
                    (beat)
I'm not such a fan of the Sushi, though... I never have
been. There is something just too fishy about food that
comes... from Davy Jones' back garden ornamental fish pond.

                                        (CONTINUED)

CONTINUED:

>   OBAMA laughs to himself.

                         OBAMA
Discussing the subject of salads, Anderson, you really
should consider... the possibility of remaining seated for
a dessert course... The juicy fruity harvested produce
salad is the best... That reminds me of a joke that Joe
once expressed to me... What was Beethoven's favorite
fruit?... It was a ba-na-na-na.

>   OBAMA laughs again.

                         OBAMA
Hey, Anderson, here are a few that I can disclose to you
without any consequence... while my daughters are not
currently... in attendance at this place... Were you ever
informed about the coffee that was filing a police
report?... It alleged that it had just... been mugged... Or
how about this one?... How many apples grow on trees?...
The answer is, of course... all of them.

>   A beat as OBAMA stops laughing
>   and sighs to himself.

                         COOPER
So, Mister President. What are your plans for the Midterms
next week?

                         OBAMA
Well, I am going to be spending the entire seven day period
of that democratic exercise... out here in the sun... My
two feet will be up... My surf will rise to a level above
its current trajectory... And my mini-bar bill will be
significantly increased within fiscally responsible
limits... for my checking account... There is a substantial
measure of political activity back at home, and it's nice
to be absent from the proceedings and... not find them a
burden.

                         COOPER
And what about Joe? Do you still hear anything from him?

>   (CONTINUED)

CONTINUED:

OBAMA

Now that is a stimulating inquiry that you put forth in
your question... I can confirm that on this occasion... We
do still exchange thoughts and words with one another both
in an electronic format... and face to face in a manner
such as we ourselves are doing at this moment...

Joe wanted to join me out here for a period, but the
problem is... Amtrak only goes so far... I have packaged
and shipped to him a parcel containing an inflatable
dolphin and a costume, however... so that he can dress up
as a choo-choo driver and then swim... the rest of the
way... Now that really would be some-fin.

                        The lights begin to fade.

OBAMA

Hey, Anderson... Here are a few more...

ACT IV, SCENE TWO | TRUMP PLAYS GOLF

                        The sound of heavy rain and
                        thunder fills a stage that is
                        dark except for brief flashes of
                        lightning.

NARRATOR
(entering)

While on vacation relaxes the nation's forty-fourth soaking
up the sun in a state of release, back home in Washington,
the pressure on his successor still only does increase.

Up early each morning is Donald J. Trump to tweet to the
world on it his thoughts. A witch-hunt, fake news, and all-
around a dishonest fake media of aughts.

But while criticism of Kavanaugh is still much in vogue,
and even though the opinions of his foreign policies is
that he's gone rogue, the President feels still that in the
upcoming election his brand remains a fighting force, and
so he retires for a day to place a round of golf upon his
Florida course.

                                            (CONTINUED)

> The NARRATOR exits as the lights
> go up on a ROOM at MAR-A-LAGO,
> where TRUMP stands by a set of
> open doors looking out at the
> heavy rain.
>
> A soaked JUNIOR enters through
> the doors carrying a paper bag.

                    JUNIOR
Okay, you know, I think that it might be raining.

                    TRUMP
Did you get them, Donald Trump Junior?

> JUNIOR holds the bag out in
> front of him.

                    JUNIOR
Two cheeseburgers with extra salad, two extra slices of
cheese, doubled up with a slice of bacon, two nuggets, and
a bed of lettuce on the top, a side of fries, a side of
nuggets with extra nuggets, holding the salad on all of
that, and two diet colas?

> TRUMP takes the bag.

                    TRUMP
Very good. All of this golf is making me very hungry.

                    JUNIOR
But you're not playing golf right now.

                    TRUMP
Fake news.

> ERIC, as wet as JUNIOR, enters
> through the same doors carrying
> a golf club.

                    ERIC
I think I wet myself.

                                        (CONTINUED)

                    TRUMP
Did you get the ball in the hole, Eric Trump?

                    ERIC
              (counting on his fingers)
One. Two. Three. Eight. Five. Seventeen shots.

                    TRUMP
Very good.

                         TRUMP pulls a scorecard from his
                         pocket.

                    TRUMP
              (to himself, writing)
Hole number one. Donald J. Trump. Seventeen.
              (to ERIC)
Now go and take your own shot.

                    ERIC
Okay. I'll be back soon.

                         ERIC exits through the doors.

                    JUNIOR
Is Eric playing himself?

                    TRUMP
He is playing me. But he is also playing for me.

                    JUNIOR
Why?

                    TRUMP
It's raining outside.

                         TRUMP takes a damp burger from
                         the bag.

                    TRUMP
Why is my burger wet?

                                             (CONTINUED)

CONTINUED:

>   JUNIOR
> It's raining outside. And I mean, why Eric? Why not someone
> who knows how to play?

>   TRUMP
> Because some people are saying that there is also thunder
> and lightning.

>   JUNIOR
> I don't get what you mean?

>   TRUMP
> Would he not be your first choice to stand outside in the
> middle of a <u>huge</u> open space with a metal golf racket during
> a thunderstorm?

>   JUNIOR
> Okay, so you know, that is a very good point. But don't you
> mean golf club?

>   TRUMP
> No. A golf club is something that is attached to a bankrupt
> hotel.

>>   A silent pause followed by a
>>   bright flash of lightning.

>   ERIC (OFF)
>   (shouting out)
> The flashy thing hurt me.

>>   There is a knock on an interior
>>   door, and CONWAY enters.

>   CONWAY
> Mister President, sir. Donald Trump Junior.

>   TRUMP
> What do you need, Kellyanne Conway?

>   CONWAY
> Another chance.

(CONTINUED)

CONTINUED:

                    TRUMP
What was that?

                    CONWAY
Senator Mitch McConnell is here to see you, sir.

                    TRUMP
Okay. Send him in.

                              CONWAY exits before a moment
                              later, MITCH MCCONNELL enters.

                    MCCONNELL
Good to see you, Comrade.

                    TRUMP
Mitch McConnell, what can I do for you?

                    MCCONNELL
I hope I'm not interrupting?

                    TRUMP
I am only playing golf.

                    MCCONNELL
Why are you inside?

                    TRUMP
Eric Trump is taking my shots for me because it is raining
outside and rain is wet. If I get wet, then my hair
multiplies, and my tan runs. It makes me look like a sad
Halloween pumpkin.

                         Beat.

                    MCCONNELL
Mister President, I am sorry to report that we may be about
to lose Texas.

                    TRUMP
What do you mean lose Texas? How can we lose something so
big?

                                                      (CONTINUED)

CONTINUED:

> MCCONNELL
> Ted Cruz is starting to look as though he's under pressure.

> TRUMP
> Is Ted Cruz the one that looks like an elderly and incontinent man who is angry because a child laughed?

> MCCONNELL
> No. That's Lindsey Graham.

> TRUMP
> Is he the one who looks like someone attempted to turn a walnut into a raisin but got bored and drew a face on it?

> MCCONNELL
> No. That's Chuck Grassley.

> TRUMP
> Is he the one who looks like a cartoon villain who has a sub-plot where he secretly collects toy dolls in a creepy way?

> MCCONNELL
> No. That's Bill Cassidy.

> TRUMP
> Is he the one who looks like every unpopular neighbor from a nineteen eight-eight sitcom who would run over your cat and then charge you for clearing their car?

> MCCONNELL
> No. That's Cindy Hyde-Smith.

> TRUMP
> Is he the one who secretly let one go in the elevator and looks really smug about it because everyone blamed Anne from human resources?

> MCCONNELL
> No. That's Marco Rubio.

> TRUMP
> Is he the one who looks like the after photo in every erectile dysfunction or hair loss infomercial ever?

(CONTINUED)

MCCONNELL
No. That's Mitt Romney.

TRUMP
Is he the one who looks like he could do you a really great
deal on that nineteen eighty-eight Toyota and can reassure
you that it is the original door, the paint just faded
faster there?

MCCONNELL
No. That's Rand Paul.

TRUMP
Is he the one who looks like he would run you down and then
tell the police that it was your fault for jaywalking, but
would then given you directions to the emergency room out
of the kindness of his heart.

MCCONNELL
No. That's Jeff Flake, and he's stepping down.

TRUMP
Is he the one who is hated by both sides?

MCCONNELL
Could you be more specific?

TRUMP
From Maine.

MCCONNELL
No. That's Susan Collins.   .

TRUMP
Is he the one who always looks as though he is surprised by
something but cannot decide if it is a good surprise or a
bad surprise?

MCCONNELL
No. That's me.

TRUMP
Who is Ted Cruz then?

(CONTINUED)

CONTINUED:

                         MCCONNELL
He's the one who thinks that holding hands should be saved
for marriage and has recently lost a bet that says he has
to grow a beard now.

                         TRUMP
Oh, Ted Cruz. I know him. Great guy. He loves me a lot.

                         MCCONNELL
I really think that he's going to need more help down
there. He's facing a real tough battle from a guy who has a
foreign-sounding name.

                         TRUMP
Are they part Cuban and born in Canada, and yet for some
reason, hate all immigrants?

                         MCCONNELL
No. That is Ted Cruz himself.

                         TRUMP
Who is it then?

                         MCCONNELL
Some guy called Beto O'Rourke.

                         TRUMP
I have never heard of him.

                         MCCONNELL
Well, neither have I. But I asked the intern who works in
my office about him, and she went bright red and said he
was a real hot dude.

                         TRUMP
So what do you --

                         MCCONNELL
She said he's a guy who has really got it going on.

                         TRUMP
What do you --

                                               (CONTINUED)

                          MCCONNELL
And that he has a sweet piece of ass on him.

                          TRUMP
What do you suggest we do?

                          MCCONNELL
I think we need to send reinforcements and fight ass to
ass. As we both know, Ted Cruz himself looks like --

                          TRUMP
A rejected cartoon villain going through a mid-life crisis.

                          MCCONNELL
Exactly.

                          TRUMP
So are you saying that we should send our own ass down
there?

                          MCCONNELL
That's right.

                          TRUMP
                       (to JUNIOR)
Donald Trump Junior, what are you doing this weekend?

                          JUNIOR
I was going to go on a hunting trip to shoot cute animals
to prove how much of a real man I am.

                          TRUMP
Cancel it. You are going to Texas.

                          JUNIOR
Am I going alone?

                          TRUMP
You can take your brother.

                              Another flash of lightning
                              followed by a pause.

                                                  (CONTINUED)

                        ERIC (OFF)

Ouch.

ACT IV, SCENE THREE | THE DEMOCRATIC PRESS CONFERENCE

> In front of a United States
> flag, a podium stands in a PRESS
> CONFERENCE ROOM somewhere in the
> CAPITOL.
>
> At the front of the scene, the
> ENSEMBLE (as PRESS) wait.

                        NARRATOR
                    (entering)

Despite worries in the South, the talk from the President
and his Senate leader remains on the line that their party
is strong, and so it is for Democrats to prepare for a
fight on all fronts to show the voters that the Republicans
are all wrong. For they seem now, a party united together
down in their trench, especially since Brett Kavanaugh took
his place upon the Supreme Court bench. While Trump's past
and his views remain most naught but obscene, a point that
Nancy Pelosi and Chuck Schumer wish to make clear when the
media convene.

> The NARRATOR exits as NANCY
> PELOSI and CHUCK SCHUMER enter.
>
> Together, they take their place
> behind the podium and begin to
> stare straight ahead without
> blinking.

                        PELOSI

Hello to the members of the press here today and all of the
American people watching at home. I am very pleased to get
the chance to speak to you all today with my good friend...

> Without her focus moving, PELOSI
> points at SCHUMER.

                        (CONTINUED)

PELOSI
The Senate Minority Leader, Senator Chuck Schumer of New
York.

SCHUMER
We are here today to tell you why you should all vote for
us, the Democrats, in next week's Midterm elections.

PELOSI
And we also have some fascinating policies that we would
like to share with you all.

SCHUMER blinks.

SCHUMER
(to PELOSI)
Oh, damn. I owe you ten dollars, Nancy.

PELOSI
Why, Chuck?

SCHUMER
I was the first to blink.

PELOSI
You owe me ten dollars, and you also owe our cuss tin ten
dollars as well.

SCHUMER
Why, Nancy?

PELOSI
You said damn.

SCHUMER
So did you.

PELOSI
That's very true. You owe me ten dollars, and we both owe
the cuss tin ten dollars each.

Beat.

(CONTINUED)

PELOSI
(to PRESS)
This here is an example of how we in the Democratic party
are always seeking to hold each other to account when we do
bad, and also how we always take responsibility for our own
actions.

SCHUMER
And holding to account is exactly what we would like to do
to Donald Trump because he is a bad person who does bad
things.

PELOSI
That's right. But he isn't the only bad person. Many of the
people that the President has surrounded himself with are
also bad people.

SCHUMER
And that is why all of America should vote for us, the
Democrats, so that we can have the power to investigate
them, the bad people, and hold them to account on behalf of
you, the people.

PELOSI
But, of course, we are not a party that is all about Donald
Trump. No, we also have plans for other things. Things like
healthcare and education. And we believe in people having
rights too.

SCHUMER
And now, we will take any questions that you may have.

PRESS #1
Hello, C-N-N here. You mentioned that you've got plans for
many things --

PELOSI
Yes. Things like healthcare.

PRESS #1
I'm just wondering if you could tell us what those plans
actually are.

                                              (CONTINUED)

                              PELOSI
Well, I like healthcare. I think that healthcare is good.

                              SCHUMER
And I think that healthcare is good too.

                              PELOSI
We are united on this cause, and that is why we are going
to work to make healthcare good for all. Does that answer
your question?

                              PRESS #1
No. Not at all.

                              PELOSI
I think we are ready for our section question now.

                              SCHUMER
                          (to PRESS #2)
Yes, you from the New York Times. Home state represent, am
I right?

                              PRESS #2
Yeah. Sure. Whatever.

                              SCHUMER
What is your question?

                              PRESS #2
You talked about wanting to hold the President to account --

                              SCHUMER
                          (nodding)
Because he does bad things.

                              PRESS #2
Are we talking impeachment here? Because that's what some
other Democrats have been suggesting.

                              PELOSI
Impeachment? Why would we need to impeach the President?

                                                        (CONTINUED)

CONTINUED:

                    SCHUMER
We would prefer to take a much more direct approach to hold
people like Donald Trump to account.

                    PELOSI
That is right. And we are prepared to do so. I have already
drafted a joint letter for us to send him so that he can
read just how much we disapprove of his actions.

                    SCHUMER
And I have bought a red pen so that I can sign that letter
in red ink. As we all know, red is the universal color of
telling someone that they are wrong.

                    PELOSI
And even more than that, I have downloaded and installed
Times Old Roman, which I used to write the letter because
it makes it look even more formal and serious than Times
New Roman.

                    SCHUMER
We are then going to send the letter through priority mail
so that he knows we are taking everything very seriously.

                    PELOSI
I think that you'll find you can't get any more direct than
that.

                    SCHUMER
And now we will take another question.

                    PRESS #3
Washington Post here.

                    PELOSI
Go ahead.

                    PRESS #3
Thank you. Together you represent the leadership of the
minority party in the world's richest and most powerful
democracy --

                    SCHUMER
You are very flattering.

                                        (CONTINUED)

PERFORMANCE LICENSE EDITION   LICENSE # _ _ _ _ _ _ _ _

                         PRESS #3
Could you really not afford to have a podium each?

                         Beat.

                         PELOSI
Apparently not.

                         SCHUMER
Next question. Yes, you...

                              Together, the voices and lights
                              fade out of the scene.

ACT IV, SCENE FOUR | THE TEXAS CAMPAIGN TRAIL

                              Somewhere in TEXAS, a LOCAL
                              walks around a CONVENIENCE
                              STORE.

                         NARRATOR
                         (entering)
Never in recent history has one election had so much at
stake, and never before has it seemed so likely that the
result will bring with it a nationwide electoral quake. For
Democrats, success is on the way, or so their supporters
indeed cry. While for Republicans, their long run in power
seems sure to dry with at least one of their majorities
soon to be nigh. Of the two, it seems the House is most
likely to flip, for the Senate class up does not favor
Chuck Schumer, not that those odds will stop one man
fighting an incumbent with his own unique brand of non-
contestable humor. It is down in the south where this
particular battle ranges strong, between one Texas state
Representative and a man living with an irrational fear of
a thong.

                              The NARRATOR exits as CRUZ
                              enters the store.

                         CRUZ
Good morning.

                                        (CONTINUED)

                              LOCAL
Morning, Mister Cruz.

                           STORE OWNER
                           (entering)
Well, darn good morning to you, Senator.

                         The STORE OWNER leads CRUZ over
                         to a nearby counter.

                           STORE OWNER
And how is our fine, generous servant of the people doing
today?

                              CRUZ
Not too good today, I'm afraid. A good law-abiding
Christian man is facing some difficulties. Farmer Moore has
had issues with foxes eating his chickens for some time
now.

                           STORE OWNER
I sure am sorry to be hearing that. Do convey to him my
thoughts and prayers.

                              CRUZ
I'll be sure to.

                           STORE OWNER
It may be a stupid question, but has he done anything to
try and fix the problem at all?

                              CRUZ
I advised him last month to get his own pet fox. You know,
only a good guy with a fox can stop a bad fox.

                           STORE OWNER
And how's that working with him?

                              CRUZ
Well, his fox became friends with the first fox, and then
they started eating the chickens together.

                           STORE OWNER
So has he got rid of the fox then?

                                             (CONTINUED)

CONTINUED:

                              CRUZ
Of course not. As I told him, if more foxes weren't the
solution, then we wouldn't have the God-given right to own
as many foxes as we want. And so he's gone and bought
himself twenty more foxes.

                              STORE OWNER
And is that working?

                              CRUZ
All of his chickens are dead. But on the bright side, he is
not the owner of the largest fox farm in the state. All
part of the great plan.

                              STORE OWNER
Many thoughts and prayers for his new endeavor.

                              CRUZ
I'll add them to my own.

                              STORE OWNER
Well, anyway, Senator, what can I get you today?

                              CRUZ
I'm going to be needing some new lead.

                              STORE OWNER
Of course.

                              CRUZ watches as the STORE OWNER
                              takes a locked box from under
                              the counter, unlocks it, and
                              then removes a single pencil.

                              STORE OWNER
Some lead for you.

                              CRUZ
That's a good joke you've got there. But I meant lead
bullets, not a lead pencil.

                              STORE OWNER
My apologies, Senator.

                                                      (CONTINUED)

>   The STORE OWNER locks the pencil
>   away again.

                          STORE OWNER
Can't be too careful now.

                          CRUZ
I'm glad you're working to keep those pencils out of the
hands of the children. We don't need them getting lead
poisoning or hitting their friends with them.

                          STORE OWNER
It's always good to see you looking out for the children,
Senator. Now, how many bullets do you be wanting?

                          CRUZ
Shall we say a round two dozen?

                          STORE OWNER
Of course.

>   The STORE OWNER reaches for a
>   small cardboard box on top of
>   the counter.

                          STORE OWNER
                       (to themselves)
Two dozen.

>   The STORE OWNER counts out the
>   bullets and goes to put the box
>   back. As they do, they knock it
>   onto the floor.

                          STORE OWNER
Darn it.

                          CRUZ
Would you like some help picking them up?

                          STORE OWNER
It's fine, Senator. I'll get around to it.

                                                      (CONTINUED)

> At the other side of the stage,
> ERIC (holding a teddy) and
> JUNIOR enter.

CRUZ

How much do I owe you?

STORE OWNER

Just twenty-four bucks.

CRUZ

Of course.

> CRUZ takes a handful of bills
> from his pocket and hands it
> over.

CRUZ

Well, I'll be seeing you.

STORE OWNER

See you later, Senator.

> The light fades on the store as
> CRUZ moves to the center of the
> stage.

ERIC

Hey, Junior.

JUNIOR

What is it, buddy?

> ERIC holds his teddy to his ear.

ERIC

I don't think teddy is well.

JUNIOR

He's a teddy, bud. He's not real.

ERIC

Then why does Betsy DeVos want school children to shoot
him?

(CONTINUED)

                              JUNIOR
She wants them to shoot big grizzly bears, not teddy bears.

                              ERIC
What's the difference?

                              JUNIOR
Well, grizzly bears go... grizzly. And teddy bears, they
go...
                    (beat, then noticing CRUZ)
Hey, there's Ted.
                    (to CRUZ)
Hey, Ted.

                              ERIC
Teddy doesn't want to talk to you. You just said he wasn't
real.

                    CRUZ walks over to them.

                              CRUZ
Hey there, Junior. Eric. I heard that you were both coming
down to help me out.

                              JUNIOR
We're at your service, Senator. Happy to be down here,
aren't we, Eric?
                    (beat)
Eric?

                              ERIC
I'm worried about teddy.

                              CRUZ
And you're right to be. Those Democrats want to silence me,
but we're going to fight them together, right?

                              ERIC
Who are you?
                    (holding up his teddy)
I'm talking about teddy. He isn't very well.

                              CRUZ
Can I take a closer look?

                                              (CONTINUED)

                              ERIC holds tighter to teddy.

                         JUNIOR
Come on, buddy. Let the nice man take a look. He might be
able to help teddy out.

                         CRUZ
That's what I'm here for. To help people wherever I can. So
long as they're a straight, white, God-fearing Christian
man who votes Republican and has never had sex before
marriage.

                         JUNIOR
I don't think Eric has had sex after marriage.

                         CRUZ
                        (to ERIC)
Come on, let me take a look at him.

                              Reluctantly, ERIC hands his
                              teddy over to CRUZ. CRUZ holds
                              it to his ear.

                         CRUZ
You're right. He doesn't sound too good, does he?

                         ERIC
He needs to go to the hospital.

                         CRUZ
                        (to JUNIOR)
Could you hold this?

                              JUNIOR takes the teddy from CRUZ
                              and holds it out as CRUZ pulls a
                              handgun from his pocket and
                              shoots the teddy's head off.

                              At the other side of the stage,
                              BETO O'ROURKE enters wearing a
                              casual suit, backward cap, and
                              carrying a skateboard.

                                                      (CONTINUED)

                         CRUZ
There you go. I've put him out of his misery.

                         ERIC
You shot teddy.

                         O'ROURKE
You monster!

                              CRUZ, ERIC, and JUNIOR turn as
                              O'ROURKE skates across the stage
                              toward them.

                         O'ROURKE
                       (to CRUZ)
How could you shoot this child's teddy in front of him like
that?

                         CRUZ
This child is thirty-four.

                         O'ROURKE
In the Republican Party, thirty-four makes someone a baby.

                         CRUZ
In the Democratic party, thirty-four makes someone still
young enough to be ripped from the womb.

                         JUNIOR
                       (to CRUZ)
Who is this guy?

                         CRUZ
This is the guy the Democrats have put up against me.

                         O'ROURKE
                       (to JUNIOR)
Yo! I'm Beto O'Rourke. What's up?

                         ERIC
Heaven. That's where teddy has gone.

                         CRUZ
If it's that bad, then I'll get teddy fixed.

                                              (CONTINUED)

CONTINUED:

                    O'ROURKE
Oh yeah? And what are you going to use to fix him? Thoughts
and prayers? Because they've fixed everything else.

                    CRUZ
They have.

                    O'ROURKE
They haven't.

                    CRUZ
They have.

                    O'ROURKE
They haven't.

                    CRUZ
They have.

                    O'ROURKE
Well, have your thoughts and prayers fix this then. Vagina.

                         A beat as CRUZ goes bright red
                         and sweaty.

                    CRUZ
                 (to JUNIOR)
Come on, Junior. I'll introduce you to the rest of my team.

                         CRUZ goes to leave with JUNIOR
                         following him.

                    JUNIOR
Come on, Eric.

                    ERIC
What about teddy?

                    JUNIOR
We'll steal you another one from a small child.

                         CRUZ, ERIC, and JUNIOR exit.

                                        (CONTINUED)

                          O'ROURKE
                    (looking after them)
Yeah, that's right. You can all get out of here.

                              O'ROURKE skates off the opposite
                              side of the stage.

ACT IV, SCENE FIVE | THE MIDTERMS

                              The stage is set as a FLORIDA
                              POLLING STATION, where the
                              ENSEMBLE (as VOTERS) cast their
                              votes. Next to them, an ELECTION
                              OFFICIAL stands by a ballot box.

                         NARRATOR
                        (entering)
November sixth, the day finally arrives. A chance for
change, not least to everyday lives. For up for contention
is the Senate's first class alongside the whole House,
giving a chance for Democrats to sweep in en masse. All
around within eyes, a sense of hope does reignite for in
the near future a vision of bright new light. Today wins
where they matter might just amount to the first real
chance to hold the President to account. And nowhere in the
nation is a race as tight as those in Florida to the south
where all sides stand close with for power a drouth.

                              The NARRATOR exits as DOOCY,
                              EARHARDT, and KILMEADE enter.

                          DOOCY
Well, hello, everyone. I'm Steve Doocy.

                        EARHARDT
That's right. You are Steve Doocy, Steve.

                          DOOCY
And you're Ainsley Earhardt, Ainsley.

                                              (CONTINUED)

                           EARHARDT
I know, Steve.
                    (to audience)
Welcome to Fox and Friends, everyone.

                           DOOCY
We're down in Florida this morning to see how all of you
are voting.

                           KILMEADE
I'm Brian, and this morning I got to meet a famous mouse in
my hotel room.

                           EARHARDT
That was a rat, Brian. And it bit you.

                              KILMEADE holds up a hand with a
                              band-aid on it.

                           KILMEADE
Look. There's a drawing of him on my band-aid.

                              COOPER enters wearing a Hawaiian
                              shirt and carrying a cocktail in
                              a coconut.

                           COOPER
I'm Anderson Cooper reporting live for C-N-N and fresh from
my vacation in Tahiti.

                              COOPER takes a drink from the
                              cocktail and begins to cough.

                           COOPER
Jesus. What do they put in this thing?

                              LESTER HOLT enters.

                           HOLT
Lester Holt for N-B-C.
                    (to COOPER)
And that, Anderson, would be tequila.

                                                    (CONTINUED)

CONTINUED:

                         COOPER
Do they do a non-alcoholic version?

                    MARTHA RADDATZ enters.

                         RADDATZ
Good morning, America. Martha Raddatz here reporting for A-
B-C. It's the Midterms. Have you planned to go out and vote
yet?

                         KILMEADE
I don't need to vote today because I voted two years ago.

                         EARHARDT
This is a different election, Brian.

                              At the back of the stage, MARCO
                              RUBIO enters and takes a ballot
                              paper from an ELECTION OFFICIAL.

                         COOPER
There is a total of thirty-five seats in the Senate being
contested right across the country today. And, of course,
one of those is right here in Florida where the incumbent
Democrat, Bill Nelson, is facing a close contest from his
Republican contender Rick Scott.

                              RUBIO marks his ballot, places
                              it in the ballot box, and then
                              goes to join DOOCY, EARHARDT,
                              and KILMEADE.

                         DOOCY
Joining us now, we have the state's incumbent Republican
Senator, Marco Rubio.

                         RUBIO
It's nice to be here. Would you all like to take a photo
together?

                         DOOCY
I'm okay.

                                        (CONTINUED)

                          EARHARDT
I'm okay too, Steve.

                          KILMEADE
I'm Brian.

                          HOLT
Of course, also up for election today are all four hundred
and thirty-five seats in the House of Representatives. This
is where the Democrats are widely expected to achieve
substantial gains and a majority.

                                   DMITRY and PETROV enter. While
                                   DMITRY distracts the ELECTION
                                   OFFICIAL, PETROV switches the
                                   ballot box with another.

                          RADDATZ
A particularly close race is also expected in Wisconsin for
the Governorship today in one of the many gubernatorial
elections taking place across America.

                                   DMITRY and PETROV take the
                                   ballot box to one side and empty
                                   it onto the floor.

                          DOOCY
What is your take on today's election, Senator Rubio?

                          RUBIO
Well, Steve, I think that we should all just be putting our
trust and faith in God and believe that he knows what he's
doing. He will see us safely through these elections with
the result that the American people deserve if we just
accept him into our lives. Most importantly, our Lord will
do as he sees fit to ensure that his words and his message
are blessed upon those who are most believing of him, and
he will provide the protection of his elected messengers
who embrace his love and use it to guide their actions.

                          DOOCY
I have no idea what you just said.

                                                        (CONTINUED)

                          RUBIO
I think the Republicans will win. Also, something about
China and shoutout to my sponsor, the N-R-A.

                          KILMEADE
I think that President Trump is going to win today.

                          EARHARDT
He isn't standing, Brian.

                          KILMEADE
That's right, folks. Donald Trump has a chair in the Oval
Office.

                          DOOCY
Senator, I'm sure we can all guess, but if I can ask, how
did you vote today?

                              PETROV picks up a ballot paper
                              and looks at it.

                          RUBIO
I voted Republican.

                          PETROV
                        (to DMITRY)
Have you see this, Dmitry. This guy wrote in Marco Rubio.

                          RUBIO
If you'd excuse me. I have to go make a table reservation
at McDonald's for tonight.

                          RUBIO exits.

                          DOOCY
He left in quite a hurry.

                          EARHARDT
He did, Steve. Which is unusual because he usually stays
around for much longer than anyone wants him to.

                          The NARRATOR enters.

                                              (CONTINUED)

NARRATOR
Six hours until the polls close.

                    As the NARRATOR exits once more,
                    the action moves to a TEXAS
                    POLLING STATION.

RADDATZ
One of the other big contests to watch closely today is
over in Texas, where Ted Cruz is facing a tough fight to be
re-elected from the Democratic challenger, Beto O'Rourke.

                    CRUZ enters and joins RADDATZ.

RADDATZ
Joining me now is Senator Cruz.
          (to CRUZ)
Senator, thank you for speaking to me.

                    At the back of the stage, a
                    MOTHER pushing a stroller enters
                    and goes to vote.

CRUZ
Very nice to be here on A-B-C today.

                    ERIC (with the stolen teddy) and
                    JUNIOR enter to join DOOCY,
                    EARHARDT, and KILMEADE.

KILMEADE
I just wet myself with excitement.

                    Beat.

HOLT
Congressman O'Rourke, the polls are showing that while you
are running a close contest, you will still be short of
securing enough votes to take the seat. How confident do
you feel that despite these numbers, you will make it over
the line?

O'ROURKE
Wussten Sie, dass ich Spanisch spreche?

                                             (CONTINUED)

                              HOLT
I'm sorry.

                            O'ROURKE
I said, did you know that I can speak Spanish?

                              HOLT
Yes, I did know that, Mister O'Rourke.

                             DOOCY
Thank you for coming on the show today, Donald Junior and
Eric.

                            EARHARDT
I thank them too, Steve.

                             JUNIOR
You know, it's great to be down here in Texas.

                            KILMEADE
I've never been to text-ass before. I have butt-dialed a
few times, though.

                         Beat.

                              ERIC
I got a new teddy.

                            O'ROURKE
Could you excuse me for a moment?

                              HOLT
Of course.

                    O'ROURKE moves close behind
                    CRUZ.

                             DOOCY
So how do you think people are voting today, Donald?

                             JUNIOR
I hope that they are voting for my father. He only wants
what is best for our country, but he needs the support of a
strong Congress that will allow him to be the…

                                       (CONTINUED)

          JUNIOR   O'ROURKE
...leader...   (shouting behind CRUZ)
                                          DILDO!

          JUNIOR
... America deserves.

                         CRUZ goes red and dabs sweat
                         from his face.

          CRUZ
          (turning to O'ROURKE)
For God's sake. Can't you stop doing that?

          O'ROURKE
Thoughts and prayers, Ted.

                         COOPER returns to the front of
                         the stage with the MOTHER.

          COOPER
And now, I can bring you an exclusive interview with a
voter who has actually met Beto O'Rourke in person.
          (to the MOTHER)
Ma'am, can you tell us where and when you first met the
Congressman?

          MOTHER
Outside five minutes ago.

          COOPER
And who did you vote for today?

          MOTHER
Ted Cruz.

                         Beat, and then the NARRATOR
                         enters.

          NARRATOR
Polls are closed.

                                                    (CONTINUED)

CONTINUED:

> The NARRATOR exits as the stage
> clears except for COOPER, DOOCY,
> EARHARDT, HOLT, KILMEADE, and
> RADDATZ.

                          HOLT
And now we come to the part of the day that all of you at
home have been waiting for.

                          RADDATZ
Stay tuned to A-B-C for the result as they come in live.

                          COOPER
And I can now confirm that America has won in Wisconsin.

                          HOLT
You can't know that yet, Anderson.

                          COOPER
Paul Ryan is stepping down.

                          RADDATZ
There is some confirmed news coming out of Wisconsin.
Democrats have taken the Governorship in the gubernatorial
race with Tony Evers winning a slim majority over
Republican incumbent Scott Walker.

                          DOOCY
And now we can go live to Sean Hannity, who is in Florida
for an update on the counting there.

                          EARHARDT
That's right, Steve. We can.

> HANNITY steps onto the stage.

                          DOOCY
How are things looking, Sean?

                          HANNITY
Get this, there isn't a result yet.

                          DOOCY
Great. We'll come back to you later.

                                              (CONTINUED)

CONTINUED:

>   HANNITY steps off the stage.

                         HOLT
More good news for the Democrats now as they are picking up
House seat after House seat this evening.

                         COOPER
With just a few more results to be announced, it's looking
as though the polls were right with the Democrats set to
reclaim control of the House of Representatives.

                         RADDATZ
Things are not going as well in the contest for the Senate,
however. It looks as though Republicans will be keeping
their control in the chamber after taking seats from the
Democrats in Indiana, Missouri, and North Dakota.

>   CRUZ and O'ROURKE reenter the
>   stage.

                         HOLT
And now, we are ready to receive the result here in Texas.
And it looks as though it is going to be a narrow win for
the incumbent Ted Cruz.

                         CRUZ
Just as God intended.
                    (to O'ROURKE)
Thoughts and prayers, Beto.

                         KILMEADE
I sometimes have thoughts.

                         O'ROURKE
                    (to CRUZ)
Orgasm.

>   CRUZ goes red and wipes sweat
>   from his face.

                         CRUZ
Will you quit doing that?

                                             (CONTINUED)

CONTINUED:

                        O'ROURKE
Period. Thong. Women's rights.

                        CRUZ
Stop it.

                    Wiping his face, CRUZ exits.

                        HOLT
And now I can get a live reaction from the runner-up here
in Texas, Beto O'Rourke.
                    (to O'ROURKE)
Congressman, how are you feeling right now?

                        O'ROURKE
It's a tight result and disappointing for myself and my
team, but now I'm going to go home, get some rest, and then
take the logical next step after losing a Senate race by
running for President.

                    O'ROURKE goes to leave.

                        O'ROURKE
Beto out y'all.

                    O'ROURKE exits.

                        DOOCY
I think that we should try to find out what's going on in
Florida again.

                        EARHARDT
I agree, Steve.

                    HANNITY steps back onto the
                    stage.

                        HANNITY
Steve. Ainsley.

                        KILMEADE
What about Brian?

                                        (CONTINUED)

                         HANNITY
What about you, Brian?

                         DOOCY
Sean, do you have any new information for us?
                    (beat)
Sean?

                         Beat.

                         EARHARDT
I think there is a delay in the satellite link, Steve.

                         HANNITY
There's no delay. We just still don't have a result yet.

                         COOPER
Florida must be a Republican victory. That's the only way
they could be so far behind the rest of the country.

                         HOLT claps as HANNITY steps back
                         offstage.

                         HOLT
You know, Anderson, that was a good one. I like that one.

                         COOPER
Really?

                         HOLT
Let's call a truce and hug it out.

                         HOLT goes to hug COOPER.

                         COOPER
Okay.

                         They hug with COOPER's back to
                         the audience as HOLT pulls out a
                         large "NBC Nightly News" sticker
                         and sticks on COOPER's back.

                                                  (CONTINUED)

CONTINUED:

                           RADDATZ
And so with the final results in it looks as though the
Democrats have done what they were widely expected to do,
with substantial gains in the House to reclaim the majority
with two hundred and thirty-five seats.

                           COOPER
Big gains for the Democrats also in the gubernatorial
contests with a net gain of seven Governorships. And --

                           DOOCY
Breaking news. The Republicans have won the Midterms by
retaining control of the Senate in a nationwide endorsement
of President Trump.

                           HOLT
I've been Lester Holt.

                           COOPER
Florida has been Florida.

                           HOLT
And that's all from me.

                           RADDATZ
And from me.

                           COOPER
And me. Good night.

                              The NARRATOR enters as the stage
                              fills with light.

                           NARRATOR
Okay, can we wrap this up here? Midterms are over, and it's
time to get back to how truly terrible everything is.

                              The stage begins to clear with
                              the ENSEMBLE helping to move
                              pieces of the set off until ERIC
                              and KILMEADE are left on stage
                              alone.

                                                    (CONTINUED)

                              At first, ERIC and KILMEADE
                              don't notice each other.

ERIC	KILMEADE
Hey, where has everyone gone?	Hey, where has everyone gone?

                              They turn and notice each other.

ERIC	KILMEADE
Who are you? I'm Eric. We should be friends. Okay. Let's be friends.	Who are you? I'm Brian. We should be friends. Okay. Let's be friends.

                              KILMEADE approaches ERIC and
                              tags him on the arm.

                        KILMEADE

Tag. You're it.

                        ERIC

I don't want to be friends anymore. I'm going and taking
teddy with me.

                              The lights fade as ERIC begins
                              to walk offstage with his head
                              down.

ACT IV, SCENE SIX | PELOSI'S PRESS CONFERENCE

                              The lights go up on a PRESS
                              CONFERENCE ROOM, where PELOSI
                              stands behind a podium
                              addressing the ENSEMBLE (as
                              PRESS, except PRESS #4).

                      NARRATOR
                      (entering)
With the voting over the Midterms bring a shock result for
President Trump and his sheep-like cult. The polls might
have shown that they were likely to lose, but they had
Russia behind them, helping voters to choose. But what does
it all mean now for Donald and his presidency coddled?
                      (MORE)
                            (CONTINUED)

CONTINUED:
NARRATOR (CONT'D)
For that is the question that many now begin to contemplate
as they feel that Democrats will soon declare checkmate or,
at the very least, his agenda frustrate. But the approach
by Pelosi seems much tamer than others in her party who
wish to take aim. And there's pressure too from voters who
believe immediate action is all that is right, and so
Pelosi is forced to address the press to prove against
Trump she is ready to fight.

The NARRATOR exits.

PELOSI
(to PRESS #2)
We've all got a lot of work to be doing, so I've only got
time to take a few short questions.

PRESS #2
Madame Representative, many in your party ran on a platform
of moving toward impeaching President Trump if Democrats
reclaimed the House. Now that you have succeeded in taking
the House back, will you commit to this action?

PELOSI
I'm not going to get drawn into that. Next question.
(to PRESS #3)
Go ahead.

PRESS #3
There is evidence to suggest that the President has already
committed what can only be described as crimes against
humanity, not least with his refusal to offer fundamental
human rights to millions, including some tens of thousands
of innocent children seeking safety. Are you sure that you
don't want to commit to impeachment?

PELOSI
I'm not going to get drawn into that. Next question.
(to PRESS #1)
Yes. New York Times.

PRESS #1
I'm actually from C-N-N.

(CONTINUED)

                              PELOSI
Well, I'm not here to get drawn into the specifics. What's
your question?

                              PRESS #1
Just a few weeks ago, alleged alcoholic sex offender Brett
Kavanaugh became the newest Justice of the Supreme Court
despite multiple allegations backed up by circumstance and
corroborating stories. His only defense was a calendar.
Given that the President nominated a man like that, don't
you think it might be time to commit to holding him to
account in the way that many in your party and many of your
voters would like to see?

                              PELOSI
Of course, I disagree with the appointment of Brett
Kavanaugh, but I'm not going to get drawn into the details.
                    (to PRESS #5)
Yes. I can take one from Fox News.

                              PRESS #5
Oh, I don't have a question. I just wanted to say thank
you.

                              PELOSI
Are there any more questions.

                              PRESS #6
I have a question.

                              PELOSI
Go ahead.

                              PRESS #6
My daughter is in third grade and has been given a home
assignment where she has to draw her favorite politician --

                              PELOSI
I'm not going to get drawn into that.
                    (beat)
Okay, are we done here? I'll be seeing you all then.

                              PELOSI exits as the PRESS shout
                              questions after her.

ACT IV, SCENE SEVEN | TRUMP'S PRESS CONFERENCE

>   The scene remains the same, and
>   the ENSEMBLE (as PRESS, except
>   PRESS #4) remain on stage as the
>   NARRATOR enters.

                          NARRATOR
Day two of a new dawn and for once the President feels a
need to set things straight somewhere other than the White
House lawn. And so the press are called to gather in the
famous East Room where Trump and his team hope to give
excuses to ensure the news agenda is just as they groom.
For shock is what settles in now they know the full result
and truth is that victory for him is seen by none except
his narrow cult. Among the media stands C-N-N's Jim Acosta
with a question on Trump's future vexed, though soon he is
to unexpectedly find his own left muscle somewhat flexed.

>   JIM ACOSTA enters.

                          ACOSTA
Jim Acosta, reporting for C-N-N.

>   ACOSTA joins the PRESS.

                          NARRATOR
But before the President can answer questions about how the
pressure on him he hopes to discount, he must first satisfy
his own boss who has arrived to ensure that any suspicious
they do surmount.

>   The NARRATOR exits.

                          PRESS #2
How much longer do you think we'll have to wait?

                          PRESS #6
I think I can hear voices.

>   From offstage, several voices
>   become audible.

                                             (CONTINUED)

                    PUTIN (OFF)
I leave for short time, and when I return, I find you lose
election.

                    TRUMP (OFF)
It was not my fault.

                              PUTIN and TRUMP enter without
                              being noticed by the PRESS.

                    PUTIN
How be it not fault of yours? How do you even lose election
that you be guaranteed to win?

                    TRUMP
It was the Democrats. They are traitors. They got help from
illegals.

                    PUTIN
I be illegals, and I help you, not them.

                              CONWAY enters.

                    CONWAY
Mister President, sir, the press are waiting for you.

                    PUTIN
Donald, you fix mess now.

                    TRUMP
Yes, Comrade Putin, sir.

                    PUTIN
Good.
                    (to CONWAY)
Kellyanne, please move ornament away from television at
home. Signal be interfering with microphone.

                    CONWAY
I'm sorry?

                    PUTIN
                    (ignoring CONWAY)
I go now.

                                        (CONTINUED)

> PUTIN points at his own eyes and
> then at TRUMP before he turns
> and exits.

CONWAY
Mister President, would you like me to go out and introduce
you first?

TRUMP
That is a great idea, Kellyanne Conway. I am glad I thought
of it.

> As CONWAY and TRUMP go to walk
> to the podium, SARAH HUCKABEE
> SANDERS enters.

HUCKABEE SANDERS
Mister President. I am here and ready to deliver this press
conference. My daddy says it's a privilege for me to do so.

TRUMP
Sarah Huckabee Sanders, where have you been for the past
ninety-four days?

HUCKABEE SANDERS
I've just been sat in my office watching documentaries on
how to care for cute little puppy dogs and also writing my
tell-all book to sell to the highest bidder. Half a million
dollars and I will shred it.

TRUMP
You have no held a press conference in three months?

HUCKABEE SANDERS
No, Mister President, I have not. I was not aware that it
was a part of my job description.

Beat.

TRUMP
Two hundred and fifty thousand, and you have a deal.

HUCKABEE SANDERS
I'm not going to take a cent less than four hundred, sir.

(CONTINUED)

CONTINUED:

                         TRUMP
We can negotiate later.

                              Together, all three walk toward
                              the podium.

                         TRUMP
                    (quietly to CONWAY)
Kellyanne Conway, I need you to go and burn that document.

                    HUCKABEE SANDERS
I've made multiple copies, Mister President.

                         TRUMP
                    (quietly to CONWAY)
Could we nuke her office?

                         CONWAY
It is right next to Mike Pence's, sir. There might be some
collateral damage.

                         TRUMP
We could leave him a memo?

                         CONWAY
I'll look into it, Mister President.

                              CONWAY exits as HUCKABEE SANDERS
                              and TRUMP reach the podium.

                    HUCKABEE SANDERS
Well, hello. Good morning to y'all, folks. My name is Sarah
Huckabee Sanders, or as my daddy calls me, Sarah Huckabee.
Y'all get it? Because he's Mike Huckabee.

                         PRESS #1
Sarah, we know who you are.

                         PRESS #3
What we want to know is why you haven't given us a briefing
in over thirteen weeks now.

                                             (CONTINUED)

HUCKABEE SANDERS
I think that is a very unfair statement and I believe that
your daddy would be very disappointed in you for saying it.
This White House has been giving daily briefings to keep
the American people updated.

PRESS #2
Where have they been? We haven't been invited.

HUCKABEE SANDERS
We outsourced them to save the American people their tax
dollars. All you have to do is turn on Fox News at nine
eastern.

PRESS #5

U-S-A! U-S-A! U-S-A!

PRESS #1
Sarah, are you talking about Sean Hannity?

TRUMP
Sean Hannity is a great man. Just ask Sean Hannity.

HUCKABEE SANDERS
And my daddy does agree. Now if there are no more
questions, then I'm going to…

HUCKABEE SANDERS   PRESS #2
... Introduce President   There's more questions!
Trump.

HUCKABEE SANDERS
(to TRUMP)
Mister President, it really is an honor for you to be with
us today.

                         HUCKABEE SANDERS stands to the
                         side as TRUMP takes the podium.

TRUMP
(pointing at PRESS #1)
Loser.
(pointing at PRESS #2)
Fake news.
(MORE)
                                                   (CONTINUED)

                        TRUMP (CONT'D)
                   (pointing at PRESS #3)
Enemy of the people.
                   (pointing at PRESS #6)
Not so great.
                   (pointing at PRESS #5)
You from Fox News, thank you for coming. It is always great
to see our free press in action. Do you have a question?

                        PRESS #5
On behalf of all of us at Fox News I wanted to congratulate
you on your election win.

                        TRUMP
That is a great question. I did great in the election, a
lot of people are saying it. My Senators did a great job.
Mitch McConnell did a great job. I did a great job, and the
result was just so great. I think that the Democrats should
learn from the Republicans that embracing their President,
that's me, okay, is the way to be great.

                        PRESS #5
You're a real hero, Mister President.

                        PRESS #3 mimes being sick.

                        TRUMP
Okay, are we done here?

                        As TRUMP turns to leave, ACOSTA
                        stands up.

                        ACOSTA
I have a question.

                        TRUMP turns back.

                        TRUMP
Who are you?

                        ACOSTA
Jim Acosta. I'm from C-N-N.

                        PRESS #1
No, I'm from C-N-N.

                                        (CONTINUED)

                         TRUMP
Okay. I will take your question so that everyone watching
can see how not so great you are.
                    (to HUCKABEE SANDERS)
Come on, let us get this guy a microphone so everyone can
hear his sad question.

                                   HUCKABEE SANDERS gestures to
                                   someone offstage. A moment
                                   later, an INTERN enters with a
                                   microphone.

                    HUCKABEE SANDERS
                      (to the INTERN)
It's okay. Like my daddy always says to me, just don't get
too close, and you'll be safe.

                         TRUMP
It is only Jim Acosta.

                    HUCKABEE SANDERS
I wasn't warning her about him, Mister President.

                                   The INTERN hands ACOSTA the
                                   microphone and stands to one
                                   side.

                         ACOSTA
I want to start with your claim that the Republicans won
the election.

                         TRUMP
It was a great result. Not so great for you at C-N-N.

                         ACOSTA
How can you claim to have won when the Democrats made
sweeping gains in gubernatorial contests right across the
country and also reclaimed the house?

                         TRUMP
Some people are saying that. You are saying that.

                         ACOSTA
I'm saying it because it's true.

                                             (CONTINUED)

                          TRUMP
Well, I do not know about that. It is what some people are
saying. I do not know who is saying it. But others are
saying we did great and they are right. Republicans won in
the Senate and did so great, okay?

                          ACOSTA
No one is saying that you didn't win the Senate --

                          TRUMP
Even you are saying it. It was a great result.

                          ACOSTA
But you didn't win the House of Representatives, and you
lost multiple Governorships.

                          TRUMP
Fake news. That is fake news, and you know it is fake news.
Do you have a real question?

                          ACOSTA
During the campaign, you consistently referred to asylum
seekers from South America as an invasion. Do you think
that you demonized them with those comments?

                          TRUMP
Fake news. All fake news. I do not even know what an asylum
seeker is. Some people do, but not me. Some people are
looking into it for me. They talk to Russia, and they talk
to North Korea. But they do that. Not me.

                          ACOSTA
Mister President, if I could just follow on --

                          TRUMP
You have had your time.

                          ACOSTA
Mister President --

                          TRUMP
Put down the microphone.
                         (to the INTERN)
Take the microphone.

                                              (CONTINUED)

CONTINUED:

                          ACOSTA
Are you worried about any of the indictments against your
allies in the Russia investigation?

                          TRUMP
I told you to shut up.

                                   The INTERN attempts to take the
                                   microphone from ACOSTA.

                          TRUMP
Hand it over.

                          ACOSTA
                     (to the INTERN)
Excuse me, ma'am.

                                   While ACOSTA holds onto the
                                   microphone, the INTERN moves
                                   over to the side, some distance
                                   from anyone else.

                                   The INTERN grabs one of their
                                   arms with the other and slaps
                                   their face before falling over.

                                   Beat.

                          TRUMP
Okay, get him out of here. Go on, get him out.

                                   HUCKABEE SANDERS grabs ACOSTA.

                          TRUMP
No one gets to treat my staff that badly except for me.

                                   HUCKABEE SANDERS aggressively
                                   drags ACOSTA offstage.

                          HUCKABEE SANDERS
Alright, you heard the President. You did bad. I'm going to
be writing to my daddy about this.

                                                  (CONTINUED)

> As he's dragged off, ACOSTA
> drops the microphone before the
> INTERN stands up, picks it up,
> and hands it to TRUMP.

                    TRUMP
Do you have any idea how long it will take her to recover?
We don't give our employees healthcare coverage.

ACT IV, SCENE EIGHT | THE GOVERNMENT SHUTDOWN

> The back of the stage remains
> dark as the NARRATOR enters.

                    NARRATOR
So begins for America a new political era, one where the
return of balance and responsibility is ever nearer. For
with the Democrats in the House, many feel that in his
office, Donald Trump is but a scared small mouse. Though
Pelosi doesn't rush to do what many wish to see, she
nevertheless ensures he knows what she thinks by sending a
handwritten decree. But when one issue comes along, she
feels a need for action more strong...

> Behind the NARRATOR, CONWAY
> crosses the stage wearing a
> protective suit without a hood.

                    NARRATOR
... For the President is demanding the building of his wall
despite the nationwide opposition calling for the project
to permanently stall. And so as Democrats together refuse
to support, the signing of any bill is what Trump decides
in response to abort. Consequences follow and beings a
nationwide shutdown, a Government inoperable all due to one
clown.

> CONWAY returns, this time
> wearing a hood and carrying a
> stick of plutonium in each hand.

                                            (CONTINUED)

                         CONWAY
                (muffled to the NARRATOR)
You should step back for the next bit.

                         NARRATOR

I'm sorry?

                              CONWAY places both sticks into
                              the same hand and uses her free
                              hand to pull off the hood.

                         CONWAY

I said you should step back for the next bit.

                         NARRATOR

Is there any reason?

                         CONWAY

I have a job to do.

                              CONWAY hands one of the sticks
                              to the NARRATOR.

                         NARRATOR

I don't need both of these, but if you hold it for long
enough, you gain super-human strength.

                              CONWAY exits as the NARRATOR
                              throws the plutonium into the
                              audience.

                         NARRATOR
                  (to audience member)
You can keep that. I don't need any more strength. I've
been carrying this administration for three and a half
acts.
                     (to audience)
And so with Federal buildings across the country all
shutting their doors, Pelosi and Schumer set off to the
White House to settle the scores.

                                                    (CONTINUED)

>   The NARRATOR exits as lights go
>   up on the OVAL OFFICE, where
>   TRUMP sits on a couch opposite
>   PELOSI and SCHUMER.
>
>   As PELOSI argues with TRUMP,
>   SCHUMER looks around with
>   interest.

PELOSI
Mister President, I think the American people recognize
that you are in the wrong here.

TRUMP
Some people are saying that, but not all people.

PELOSI
You can't expect us to fund the building of an unnecessary
monument to racism at the expense of hardworking Americans.

TRUMP
We need to build that wall, Nancy Pelosi. There are a lot
of illegal and bad people, some say criminal people, who
want to do us bad.

PELOSI
That isn't true, Mister President.

TRUMP
It is true, I know many of them personally.

PELOSI
Mister President, we are not going to agree to build this
wall.

TRUMP
It is not up to you, I am the President.

PELOSI
If I impeach you and Mike, then I will be the President.

TRUMP
No. Paul Ryan would be the President.

                                              (CONTINUED)

CONTINUED:

                         PELOSI
Paul Ryan will soon be nothing but a departed stain on our
democracy.

                         TRUMP
Paul Ryan is a great --

                              At the back of the stage, the
                              desk swivels around to reveal
                              PAUL RYAN on the reverse.

                         RYAN
I really wish people would stop saying my name three times
in a row. I was trying to stop some raccoons from eating my
car. Second time this week.
                         (beat)
How do I get out of this place?

                         PELOSI
You never will. This will follow you for the rest of your
life.

                         TRUMP
                    (pointing offstage)
Through that door and then go right.

                         RYAN
How far do I go right?

                         TRUMP
Never stop.

                              RYAN exits as PENCE enters from
                              the other side of the stage.

                         PENCE
Mister President, why is there a gas mask and some burn
cream on my desk.

                              A loud band accompanies a flash
                              of bright orange and green light
                              from offstage.

                                             (CONTINUED)

CONTINUED:

                         TRUMP
Mike Pence. You are going to need a new office.

                         PELOSI
This is just another example of how you have no sense of
moderation.

                         PENCE sits down next to TRUMP.

                         TRUMP
You are just jealous because you are a loser.

                         PELOSI
I won the House.

                         TRUMP
I won the White House.

                         PELOSI
The White House belongs to the American people.

                         TRUMP
The American people love me.

                         PELOSI
No, Russia loves you.

                         PENCE
I think that is an unfair statement. God also loves him.

                         TRUMP
And Mike Pence would know. He is good friends with God.

                         PELOSI
I think that Chuck might want to say something here.

                         A beat as PELOSI, PENCE, and
                         TRUMP all turn to SCHUMER.

                         SCHUMER
It's a nice place you have here.

                                              (CONTINUED)

                                     Another beat and then the
                                     arguing resumes as green smoke
                                     begins to appear from the wings.

ACT IV, SCENE NINE | HAMBERDERS & FRIES

                                     The stage is dark as the
                                     NARRATOR enters.

                              NARRATOR
Unresolved is how in the weeks that follow, all problems
remain, and always the other side is to blame is what both
continue to claim.

                          TRUMP (IN DARKNESS)
                              (quietly)
/WHO WOULD HAVE GUESSED, THAT I'M SO BLESSED? SO MANY
NUGGETS HERE TO TEST./

                              NARRATOR
And so the problems caused by the Government closure only
intensify so that even the President is forced to suffer
some exposure.

                          TRUMP (IN DARKNESS)
                              (quietly)
/BEEF BERDER. CHEESE ON TOP. SOMETHING WITH FISH TO TOP THE
LOT. I CALL AND HAVE DELIVERED, A CULINARY COVFEFE./

                              NARRATOR
For as one sporting trophy finds a new shelf to call home,
Donald Trump invites the team to the place he alone calls
his Rome.

                          TRUMP (IN DARKNESS)
                              (quietly)
/I AM A JOKE. I AM A TRICK. I LIKE BIG WALLS MADE OF
BRICKS. AND IF YOU VOTE FOR ME, IT IS WHAT YOU WILL
REGRET./

                                                      (CONTINUED)

                            NARRATOR
But with a meal planned and no chef on hand, the President
is forced to pick up his phone and order in berders, all to
be served upon silver-plated servers.

                                        The NARRATOR exits as lights go
                                        up on the WHITE HOUSE DINING
                                        ROOM.

                                        TRUMP sits alone at a long
                                        table.In front of him, fast food
                                        is spread out on silver plates.

                            TRUMP
/SO MUCH TREASON STILL TO DO. DO I HAVE ONE SON OR IS IT
TWO? WHERE ARE MY GUESTS? WHERE ARE MY GUESTS? WHERE ARE MY
GUESTS?/

                                        TRUMP looks around at the empty
                                        chairs.

                            TRUMP
                          (to no one)
Have you tried the hamberders? They are so great.

                                        TRUMP stands and goes to sit at
                                        another of the chairs.

                            TRUMP
I agree. They are so great. I am a big fan of all of the
hamberders. I love the hamberders, and they love me.

                                        Again, TRUMP stands and goes to
                                        sit at another chair.

                            TRUMP
Does anyone have any fries? I love fries. A big fan of the
fries.

                                        TRUMP stands and sits at another
                                        chair, this time grabbing a cup
                                        of fries in front of him.

                                                        (CONTINUED)

CONTINUED:

                    TRUMP
I have some fries.

                         TRUMP moves back to the previous
                         chair.

                    TRUMP
I will trade you six nuggets and a Berder King for some
fries.

                         TRUMP moves back again.

                    TRUMP
I will not take anything less than nine nuggets and a
barbecue cheeseberder.

                         TRUMP moves back to the other
                         chair.

                    TRUMP
How about a side salad?

                         TRUMP moves back once more.

                    TRUMP
               (to no one next to him)
Do you hear this guy? This guy wants to trade a side salad
for some fries.

                         TRUMP moves to the next chair
                         along to respond.

                    TRUMP
Sad. Such a bad deal. It should be nothing less than two-
quarter pounders with cheese.

                         TRUMP returns to the first
                         chair.

                    TRUMP
There is no need to fight. I am a generous man. Some say
the most generous. There is plenty of berders for all. Just
remember that you all owe me fifteen dollars. Now, who
wants a diet cola?

                                             (CONTINUED)

                         ERIC and JUNIOR.

                              ERIC
Hey, dad, can we have some food?

                              TRUMP
This is not food for you, Eric Trump. This is food for the
Clemson Tigers.

                              JUNIOR
So you know, it seems strange that they haven't arrived
yet.

                              TRUMP
They are on their way, Donald Trump Junior. They called me
to say they are stuck in traffic.

                              JUNIOR
When did they call?

                              TRUMP
Three days ago.

                         Beat.

                              JUNIOR
Are you sure that they're coming?

                              TRUMP
They will be here soon. Why would they not come? There is
so much great food. Great American food that is waiting for
them. We have some great American berders and also some
great American fries from France.

                              JUNIOR
Dad, it's eleven P-M.

                         CONWAY enters.

                              CONWAY
Mister President, the coach of the Clemson Tigers just
called, and he said he's sorry, but the team can't make it
tonight because...

                                              (CONTINUED)

>   CONWAY pulls a memo out from her
>   pocket.

                              CONWAY
                         (reading memo)
"Just make something up yourself and tell him that. Our
hamster died or something like that."

                              TRUMP
Kellyanne Conway, find out which of the players voted for
me and send them my condolences. It must be hard when so
many hamsters die at once.

                              CONWAY
I think only one hamster died, sir.

                              TRUMP
                         (to JUNIOR and ERIC)
Donald Trump Junior. Eric Trump. Help me eat this food.

>   There is a knock on a door, and
>   HUCKABEE SANDERS enters carrying
>   a box of office supplies and a
>   desk plant.

                         HUCKABEE SANDERS
Mister President, I have come to hand in my resignation. I
really feel that it is time for me to leave. You know, my
daddy always taught me that when your boss has your office
nuked, you should take it as a sign to move on.

>   TRUMP stands.

                              TRUMP
Who are you?

                         HUCKABEE SANDERS
I'm Sarah Huckabee Sanders, Mister President. My daddy is
Mike Huckabee.

                              TRUMP
                         (to CONWAY)
Kellyanne Conway, what did she do here?

                                                  (CONTINUED)

CONTINUED:

                        CONWAY
She was your press secretary, Mister President.

                        TRUMP
                  (to HUCKABEE SANDERS)
I have never met you before, but some people say that you
did a great job. You had a real honor to work for me.

                        HUCKABEE SANDERS
Thank you, Mister President, I hope that...

                              Ignoring HUCKABEE SANDERS, TRUMP
                              sits back at the table and turns
                              to JUNIOR.

                        HUCKABEE SANDERS
... despite recent --

                        TRUMP
                  (to JUNIOR)
Now tell me, how long have you been playing football?

ACT IV, SCENE TEN | COUNTDOWN TO 2020

                              The NARRATOR enters a dark
                              stage.

                        NARRATOR
And so pass further weeks and with them more issues mount
en masse with no clear way through the legislative impasse.
But then finally comes a break when Democrats pass measures
to allow the Government to rewake.

Meanwhile, the President claims he has a new plan to build
his wall, one that would keep his rivals from having any
final call. But he makes a mistake when an emergency he
declares for Congress are ready to remind him that the
issue is still very much within their own affairs.

And all the while just nearby a new fight kicks off, for
the Democrats now have a twenty-twenty nomination standoff.
                        (MORE)

                                        (CONTINUED)

CONTINUED:

NARRATOR (CONT'D)

All around names are thrown, and many candidates step in,
all hoping to prove that this is a race where they have
skin.

> The NARRATOR exits as the lights
> go up on a ROOM IN THE WHITE
> HOUSE, where TRUMP sits watching
> a giant TV. In the giant TV,
> HANNITY.

HANNITY
(mid-show)

Coming up next, we're going to be looking at Nancy Pelosi's
secret plan to let more hurricanes onto American soil. But
first, get this, it's the advertisements.

> HANNITY exits to the replaced by
> ELIZABETH WARREN.

WARREN

Alight. Let's do this. Hi, I'm Elizabeth Warren, and I'm
running to be your next President. Whatever your problem
is, you can trust that I have a plan for that. Perhaps
you're late for a party and have nothing to take? Give me a
call, and I'll bake you a flan for that. Feeling hungry in
the morning? Eat some bran for that. Lost your wedding ring
in some dirt? I'll come along and help you pan for that.

TRUMP

Sad. What else is on?

> TRUMP presses a button on a
> remote, and WARREN exits to be
> replaced by JOE BIDEN.

BIDEN

Hello, I'm Joe Biden, and I'm running for President. You
may remember me from Barack Obama.

TRUMP

More sad.

> TRUMP presses again, and BIDEN
> exits as WARREN reenters.

(CONTINUED)

                    WARREN
Perhaps you're a straight woman looking for a date? Hi, I'm
Elizabeth Warren, and if this sounds like you, I can find
you a man for that. Not sure what to wear on that date? I
recommend something in cyan for that.

                    TRUMP
Not great.

                         TRUMP presses again, and WARREN
                         exits to be replaced by BERNIE
                         SANDERS.

                    SANDERS
Yes. It's me, Bernie Sanders. I am still here, I am not
dead, and I am ready to shout even louder than before. Now,
listen up. I know that many of you think that I helped get
President Trump elected, but here are the facts, we are
going to have a **REVOLUTION!**

                    TRUMP
Why do anyone prefer this guy?

                         TRUMP presses again, and SANDERS
                         is replaced by WARREN.

                    WARREN
Hi, I'm a woman...

                    TRUMP
That is why.

                    WARREN
... and are you feeling tired after a long day at work? I
sleep in a divan for that. Or do you just need to let out
some stress by complaining about the boss? Get a friend
called Ann for that.

                    TRUMP
Why is everything advertisements?

                                              (CONTINUED)

>   TRUMP presses again, and WARREN
>   exits to be replaced by the
>   NARRATOR as 1950's comedy music
>   begins to play.

                    NARRATOR (OFF)
                  (as a voiceover)
Coming soon. The world knows here to be the chief aid to
the President while the world knows him to burn her boss
while she's at work...

                      TRUMP
I like this show.

                    NARRATOR (OFF)
... But what really goes on behind closed doors? Find out
in our brand new sitcom, The Conways.

>   A light finds GEORGE CONWAY sat
>   at a kitchen table typing on a
>   laptop.

                      GEORGE
                    (typing)
"The President is a danger to our nation, and we should all
be scared of what he might do next. L-O-L." And tweet.

>   Canned laughter followed by the
>   sound of a door opening.

                    CONWAY (OFF)
Hey, George. I'm home.

                      GEORGE
                  (to audience)
Oh. I better put my laptop away, or she'll want to see my
search history.

>   More canned laughter as GEORGE
>   puts the laptop to one side, and
>   CONWAY enters.

                                              (CONTINUED)

                              CONWAY
Now, George, I hope that you weren't looking at anything
you shouldn't have been while I was at work.

                              GEORGE
Only a --

                                        As GEORGE is interrupted by a
                                        beep, he winks to the audience
                                        before more canned laughter
                                        plays.

                              CONWAY
Oh, George.

                                        The light on CONWAY and GEORGE
                                        go down as the music stops.

                           NARRATOR (OFF)
                         (as a voiceover)
Staring Kellyanne Conway and her husband George Conway as
they try to make their personal lives work despite their
professional lives.

                                        Light up on the table where
                                        CONWAY and GEORGE sit eating.

                              CONWAY
                             (cooly)
So, I heard what you said about the President today.

                              GEORGE
This sauce seems mild.

                              CONWAY
I thought that you'd had enough spice for today in your
tweets, George.

                              GEORGE
Can you pass me the pepper?

                              CONWAY
Get your own pepper, George.

                                                     (CONTINUED)

CONTINUED:

                    NARRATOR (OFF)
                  (as a voiceover)
The Conways, next Thursday, nine eastern.

                         The light on CONWAY and GEORGE
                         goes down as the NARRATOR exits.

                    TRUMP
Such a great show. It would be, I am in it.

                         WARREN returns.

                    WARREN
Hi, I'm Elizabeth Warren, and if you're looking for a
European city vacation, then I recommend you visit Milan
for that. Or, if you want a more cultural experience, then
why not visit Japan for that? Worried how you'll be able to
afford it? Well, under my plan, the rich won't keep getting
richer, and you'll earn more.

                    TRUMP
Fake news.

                         TRUMP presses a button again,
                         and WARREN exits to be replaced
                         by GENERIC WHITE MAN.

                    GENERIC WHITE MAN
Hi, I'm Mike Bloomberg, and I'm richer than Donald Trump.

                    TRUMP
Wait, what did that woman say?

                         TRUMP presses again, and GENERIC
                         WHITE MAN exits to be replaced
                         by OBAMA.

                    OBAMA
Good sundown to you all... I am erstwhile President, Barack
Obama, and I would like to take this occasion to tell you
all about my new venture... Barack Obama Greeting Cards...
At Barack Obama Greeting Cards, you can always find... a
printed material with a message... that is just right.

                                        (CONTINUED)

CONTINUED:

                              OBAMA puts his hand to his heart
                              and looks longingly into the
                              distance.

                       OBAMA
For Saint Valentines' day.
                 (romantically)
My dear, my heart beats in a most irregular pattern...
whenever I think of the person whom you are... I have a
deep infatuation and appreciation of yourself... and I feel
amorousness... in your specific direction.

                       OBAMA looks forward once more.

                       OBAMA
For birthdays.
                 (cheerful)
Happy birthday to you... Happy birthday to you... Happy
anniversary of the joyful day... on which you were born and
began to make... your contribution to our world... Happy
birthday to you.

                       OBAMA looks down thoughtfully.

                       OBAMA
For bereavement
                 (sincere)
At this most difficult of times... I pass on thoughts most
forthright and genuine on behalf of myself... and my
wife... slash husband... slash partner... slash
girlfriend... slash boyfriend... slash housemate... slash
goldfish.

                       OBAMA looks forward.

                       OBAMA
And for Christmas... Happy Holidays.
                 (beat)
Barack Obama Greeting Cards... Why say something in three
words when you could say it in thirty-three?

                       TRUMP
                 (to himself)
What the hell was that?

                                (CONTINUED)

> The lights on the scene fade.

ACT IV, SCENE ELEVEN | THE DEMOCRATIC DEBATE

> A DEBATE STAGE where a spotlight
> shines upon an unoccupied desk.
> Behind the desk, two chairs.

NARRATOR
(entering)
And so as focus moves to the year ahead, for Democrats, the
time has come to decide which of them forward dares to
tread. With the next election now just twelve months away,
voters begin to pray as thoughts turn eager to know who has
it in them to deal the Trump presidency its final blow.

At the start, over twenty names went in, but not all can go
on as they hope to begin. But how to narrow down to those
au fait? The answer lies in a live debate presented
televised and who better to host than M-S-N-B-C who sent
their anchors who stand tall foremost. First, to cut
through the lies and help the field narrow, ordinarily live
each night, it's Rachel Maddow.

> RACHEL MADDOW enters and waves
> to the audience as she stands
> next to the NARRATOR.

MADDOW
Good evening.

NARRATOR
And to stand alongside and help you see at which candidates
to nod, it's the network's --

> CHUCK TOOD enters and stands at
> the opposite side.

TODD
Chuck Todd.

NARRATOR
Yes. I was just about to get to that.

(CONTINUED)

                              TODD
Carry on.

                            NARRATOR
And so with the stage all set, it's time to place that
final bet on who will come out top and whose campaign is
set to suffer a humiliating electoral flop.

                    The NARRATOR exits.

                            MADDOW
Hello. I'm Rachel --

                              TODD
And I'm Chuck Todd.

                            MADDOW
Welcome to this, the first Democratic debate for --

                              TODD
And now, let's meet the candidates who will be debating
tonight.

                            MADDOW
First up, it's Vermont Senator, Bernie Sanders.

                                   A light shines on the first of
                                   eight podiums. Stood behind it,
                                   SANDERS.

                            SANDERS
Yes. Hello. I am here, and tonight I will be talking so
loud that you will still hear me at home even if you mute
your television.

                    The light fades.

                              TODD
The junior Senator from the state of California, Kamala
Harris.

                                   A light shines on the second
                                   podium where KAMALA HARRIS is
                                   standing.

                                             (CONTINUED)

CONTINUED:

                         HARRIS
Yes, hello. Tonight, I'm going to make Joe Biden wish that
he didn't turn up.

                         The light fades.

                         MADDOW
Yes, hello. Tonight, I'm going to make Joe Biden wish that
he didn't turn up.

                              A light shines on the third
                              podium where BIDEN is standing.
                              Noticing the audience, he smiles
                              and shoots his fingers out.

                         BIDEN
Did you miss me?

                         The light fades.

                         TODD
Mayor of South Bend Indiana, Pete Buttigieg.

                              A light shines on the fourth
                              podium where PETE BUTTIGIEG
                              stands.

                         BUTTIGIEG
Remember, America, if you vote for me, then Mike Pence will
cry real tears.

                         The light fades.

                         MADDOW
Author and former independent candidate for the House,
Marianne Williamson.

                              A light shines on the fifth
                              podium where MARIANNE WILLIAMSON
                              stands.

                         WILLIAMSON
Nineteen seventy-three called. They want us to bring back
the love, y'all.

                                        (CONTINUED)
PERFORMANCE LICENSE EDITION   LICENSE # _ _ _ _ _ _ _ _

CONTINUED:

                        The light fades.

                         TODD
Democratic candidate in the two thousand and eighteen
Senate race in Texas, Beto O'Rourke.

                         A light shines on BETO O'ROURKE
                         stood behind the sixth podium.

                         O'ROURKE
I am ready to kill this thing.

                         The light fades.

                         MADDOW
Massachusetts Senator, Elizabeth Warren.

                         WARREN
Let's do this together. And after that, let's do it again.
And after that, I have signed photos of my dog to give to
all of you.

                         The light fades.

                         TODD
Representing Ohio's thirteenth district, Tim Ryan.

                         A light shines on the final
                         podium where GENERIC WHITE MAN
                         stands.

                         GENERIC WHITE MAN
Hello.

                         The light fades.

                         MADDOW
Former Colorado Governor, John Hickenlooper.

                         The light on GENERIC WHITE MAN
                         returns.

                         GENERIC WHITE MAN
Hi.

                                        (CONTINUED)

                         The light fades.

                    TODD
Also from the state of Colorado, Senator Michael Bennet.

                         The light on GENERIC WHITE MAN
                         returns.

                    GENERIC WHITE MAN
How you doing?

                         The light fades.

                    MADDOW
Mayor of New York City, Bill DeBlasio.

                         The light on GENERIC WHITE MAN
                         returns.

                    GENERIC WHITE MAN
Good to see you.

                         The light fades.

                    TODD
Former representative of Maryland's Sixth Congressional
District, John Delaney.

                         The light on GENERIC WHITE MAN
                         returns.

                    GENERIC WHITE MAN
Thanks for coming.

                         The light fades.

                    MADDOW
He's currently representing the sixth Congressional
District, this time in Massachusetts, Seth Moulton.

                         The light on GENERIC WHITE MAN
                         returns.

                                             (CONTINUED)

CONTINUED:

                         GENERIC WHITE MAN
Great to be here.

                              The light fades.

                         TODD
Governor Steve Bullock of Montana.

                                   The light on GENERIC WHITE MAN
                                   returns.

                         GENERIC WHITE MAN
Good evening.

                              The light fades.

                         MADDOW
Former mayor of New York City and billionaire, Michael
Bloomberg.

                                   The light on GENERIC WHITE MAN
                                   returns.

                         GENERIC WHITE MAN
I'm excited to be here tonight.

                              The light fades.

                         TODD
Former Senator from the state of Alaska, Mike Gravel.

                                   The light on GENERIC WHITE MAN
                                   returns.

                         GENERIC WHITE MAN
Remember me?

                              The light fades.

                         MADDOW
Billionaire hedge fund manager, Tom Steyer.

                                   The light on GENERIC WHITE MAN
                                   returns.

                                             (CONTINUED)

GENERIC WHITE MAN
I am privileged to be here. No, really, I am **privileged** to
be here.

The light fades.

TODD
Washington Governor, Jay Inslee.

The light on GENERIC WHITE MAN
returns.

GENERIC WHITE MAN
What's happening.

The light fades.

MADDOW
And finally, former House Representative from the state of
Pennsylvania, Joe Sestak.

The light on GENERIC WHITE MAN
returns.

GENERIC WHITE MAN
Yeah. I've got nothing.

The light fades.

TODD
There are, of course, several candidates who were not able
to join us up on the stage tonight. The first of these is
Tulsi Gabbard from Hawaii, who refused her invitation after
hearing that there might be some Democrats here.

MADDOW
Julián Castro and Cory Booker, who, despite being two of
the most experienced and qualified candidates in this race,
are neither white billionaires or Pete Buttigieg.

TODD
And Andrew Yang who is here tonight, but is currently busy
handing out free money to strangers on the sidewalk.

(CONTINUED)

                              MADDOW
Well, you've met all of the candidates, and now it's their
time to debate.

                                        Lights go up on all eight
                                        podiums as MADDOW and TODD take
                                        their places behind the desk.

                              MADDOW
Tonight, we are going to be covering some of the major
issues that people right across America care about. Climate
change, international relations, and the economy will all
be up for discussion this evening.

                              TODD
And after that, we will follow up by ignoring many of the
other issues that people care about and bring the level of
discourse down to that of a high school debating society.

                              MADDOW
We're going to begin tonight with Elizabeth Warren.
                         (to WARREN)
Senator Warren --

                              WARREN
Yeah. I'm ready for this.

                              MADDOW
Senator, since you launched your campaign for President,
you have announced plans to offer free college, free child
care, healthcare for all, cancel existing student debt,
introduce new taxes on the wealthiest, new regulations to
protect everyday consumers, and also to break up major
corporations so that they can't exploit their position. So
my question is, who are you going to be choosing as a
running mate?

                              WARREN
That is an excellent question, and I think that it's great
that you're asking it. But if you don't mind, I'd like to
answer it while I get in my daily exercise.

                                                      (CONTINUED)

> WARREN moves to the center of
> the stage and begins a series of
> exercises.

SANDERS

Is she allowed to do that?

WARREN

It would be great if you came over to join me, Bernie.

SANDERS

I'm okay. I put my back out while trying to open the window
in my hotel room so I could keep cool.

WARREN

In my room, I have a fan for that.

HARRIS

I put my back out carrying the knowledge that there are
still millions of disadvantaged Americans right across our
country who are not being given the rights that they're
entitled to.

BIDEN

I know Barack Obama.

MADDOW

If I can, I would like to get an answer from Senator Warren
on my first question before we move onto any other subject.

WARREN

So, I've not really given it much thought yet, but I know
that it needs to be someone who cares about this country
just as much as I do. It needs to be someone who wants to
see everyone get the opportunities they deserve and who
wants to see accountability for those in power...

> WARREN begins doing a series of
> push-ups.

WARREN

... It needs to be someone who, just like me, will always
keep pushing for what is right.

(CONTINUED)

>   WARREN does a final push-up
>   before standing, rubbing her
>   hands together, and returning to
>   her podium.

                              TODD
Senator Harris.

                              HARRIS
Yes, that's me. America may remember me my many appearances
in the Senate. I'm the one who makes Republicans weep like
a small child.

                              TODD
Senator, do you think that the economy is working for
everyday people?

                              HARRIS
No, I do not. Not at all. And let me tell you why. When I
travel around America, I meet people who are struggling to
put food on the table for their children even though they
are working two or more jobs. And why does this happen? It
happens because in America, the system isn't fair and
wealth and opportunity is being disproportionately hoarded
by billionaires --

                              TODD
I'd just like to bring in billionaire Tom Steyer.

                         GENERIC WHITE MAN
Oh, I... It's nice to be here today.

                              HARRIS
If I could just add. When I go around and talk to families,
that person who is going around, that person is me.

                              MADDOW
Senator Bernie Sanders. The environment, what's your plan?

                              SANDERS
I have lots of plans, Rachel. I have plans for everything.
The economy, there's a plan for that. Trade, there's a plan
for that. Infrastructure, there's a plan for that.
                              (MORE)

                                                   (CONTINUED)

SANDERS (CONT'D)

And if you vote for Bernie Sanders on Super Tuesday, you can get all of my plans for the price of just one plan. But hurry, this offer is only good for one election cycle and perhaps another after that. And remember, you cannot pay for Bernie Sanders in installments. Some people did not seem to understand that last time. You must vote for me all at once, not some in twenty-sixteen and some in twenty-twenty.

MADDOW

Senator, I asked about the environment. What is your plan for climate change?

SANDERS

We are going to have a revolution!

MADDOW

But specifically, how are you going to tackle the climate crisis?

SANDERS
(shrugging)
Point at a bush and then shout at a tree.

TODD

Beto O'Rourke.

O'ROURKE

Yo. Or as we say in Spanish, yo.

TODD

Mister O'Rourke, you are currently polling at just three percentage points in this race.

O'ROURKE

Yes. What is my question?

TODD
(to BIDEN)
Vice President Biden.

SANDERS
(pointing at O'ROURKE)
Hold on. I have a question for this guy.

(CONTINUED)

                              TODD
Okay, well, go ahead, Senator Sanders.

                              SANDERS
Thank you.
                    (to O'ROURKE)
Are you actually a real person?

                              O'ROURKE
Hey, cool it, gramps. No need to get personal.

                              SANDERS
Gramps? Who are you calling gramps? Back in my day, if I
had called someone gramps, they would have said no, I'm
your grandmother. Have you thought about wearing glasses,
Bernie?

                              TODD
Vice President Biden.

                              BIDEN
Yes. I'm ready.

                              TODD
I'd like to yield my time over to the Senator from
California.

                    HARRIS clears her throat.

                              BIDEN
I'm no longer ready.

                              HARRIS
Thank you, Chuck.
                    (to BIDEN)
Now, Joe, I am about to take you to school. Which is a lot
more than you did for all those children, including myself,
when you opposed bussing.

                              BIDEN
Is it time yet?

                              TODD
Not yet, Vice President.

                                        (CONTINUED)

>   WARREN pulls a bag of popcorn
>   from her pocket and begins to
>   eat as HARRIS turns to her.

                    WARREN
Would you like some?

                    HARRIS
Very kind of you.

>   HARRIS takes a handful of
>   popcorn and turns back to BIDEN.

                    HARRIS
Joe, I do not think that you are a racist. But I am going
to spend the next few minutes making everyone watching at
home think that you might be.

>   BIDEN turns to the audience and
>   smiles.

                    HARRIS
Do you remember that time that you openly defended and
called your friends, two racist Senators? Because I do
remember that.

>   BIDEN's smile turns into a
>   frown.

                    WARREN
This is so good to watch.

>   HARRIS turns to WARREN.

                    WARREN
You go, sister.

                    HARRIS
Can I get the recipe for that popcorn? It's good stuff.

                    WARREN
Sure, I'll send it to you later. We should put toffee in
the next batch to mark the occasion of Joe being in a
sticky situation.

                                            (CONTINUED)

                         HARRIS and WARREN high five.

                    WARREN
I do try.

                    TODD
Vice President Biden, would you like to respond to Senator
Harris?

                    BIDEN
Yes, I would.
                    (to HARRIS)
Now you listen to me. You're acting like a child and
talking about things that you don't understand --

                    HARRIS
Joe --

                    BIDEN
No, you're going to listen to me --

                    HARRIS
Mister Vice President --

                    BIDEN
I simply cannot be a racist. Some of my best friends are
Barack Obama.

                    Beat.

                    TODD
Senator Harris, would you like to add anything?

                    HARRIS
I don't think that I need to.

                    MADDOW
Senator Warren. Healthcare, what is your plan?

                    WARREN
My plan is straightforward. I believe that healthcare is
one of our human rights and that all of us are human. Even
Donald Trump.
                         (MORE)

                                        (CONTINUED)

                          WARREN (CONT'D)
We need to cut out the insurance companies and the profit
that they make and ensure that no one else ever goes broke
because they needed care.

                            MADDOW
And what do you say to those who think that your plan will
take choice away from patients and perhaps force them to
seek care from professionals they don't know or trust?

                            WARREN
I believe that we need to build a system where we can all
have trust in those who are caring for us. It's essential
for us all to have confidence and trust in our doctors. You
should always be able to open with them. You should be able
to tell them if you're a Republican, for example. There is
no cure for that, but at least they can laugh at you too.

                            MADDOW
It's nice to see that you're able to show a sense of humor.
It's something we've certainly not seen much from our
current President.

                            WARREN
Well, having a sense of humor while working tirelessly to
make our world a better place? That's precisely what strong
and independent women from Massachusetts do. And I'll tell
you what else we do. We also run for President.

                        Beat.

                            BIDEN
I know Elizabeth Warren.

                            MADDOW
And finally, if I could just ask one more question. Can you
tell us what distinguishes your plans for healthcare from
those of Bernie Sanders and Joe Biden?

                            WARREN
That's an easy one. Unlike Bernie's plans, I actually know
how to pay for mine. And unlike Joe's, mine actually exist.

                            MADDOW
Thank you, Senator Warren.

                                            (CONTINUED)

                          TODD
Marianne Williamson. On behalf of everyone watching, what
are you actually doing here?

                          WILLIAMSON
What am I doing here? What are you doing here? What are we
all doing here? Do any of us truly know our purpose? Do we
have a purpose, or are we destined to float through time as
a collection of linked atoms brought together by our desire
to move forward and do with our existence things that those
before us were not able to achieve with their own?

                          SANDERS
This is like listening to Marco Rubio if he joined the
Church of Scientology.

                          MADDOW
Mayor Pete Buttigieg. Many believe that your campaign is
facing a significant problem in attracting the support of
minority voters. What do you have to say to that?

                          BUTTIGIEG
I would say that they are correct.

                          MADDOW
Okay, but do you have a plan to bring this significant
number of voters onto your side?

                          BUTTIGIEG
I think that we need to be doing more to stop racism in
this country. We need to call our racists. Donald Trump,
our President, is a racist.

                          MADDOW
But what are you actually going to do?

                          BUTTIGIEG
I think that we should take white people and introduce
black people to them.

                          Beat.

                          MADDOW
Would you like another go?

                                                        (CONTINUED)

                         BUTTIGIEG
I'm probably good.

                          HARRIS
No, go on. Try again.
                    (to WARREN)
Have you got any more of that popcorn?

                          WARREN
I'd subscribe to H-B-O for content like this.

                    HARRIS and WARREN high five.

                         BUTTIGIEG
I have no problem with black or minority voters. They just
have a problem with me.

                          MADDOW
Okay, well, we'll move on. Actually, you know what, I've
got a question for any of the men here tonight. This
question is open to any of you. What makes you qualified to
make decisions on behalf of millions of women across
America?

                          Beat.

                          MADDOW
Nothing. No one has any answer to that?

                     GENERIC WHITE MAN
If I could just talk?

                          MADDOW
No one is interrupting you, Representative --

                     GENERIC WHITE MAN
I would prefer it if my name wasn't on the record here.

                          MADDOW
Okay, well, go ahead. What do you have to say?

                                              (CONTINUED)

                           GENERIC WHITE MAN
I just want to say that I know women. I respect women. I
have, in fact, met women. My wife, for example, is a woman.
I have also read about women.

                              BIDEN and SANDERS drink from two
                              glasses of water.

                              WARREN
If I could just interrupt. I'd just like to say that I am
actually an expert in this area as I do, in fact, have a
vagina.

                              BIDEN and SANDERS spit their
                              water out.

                              SANDERS
Is she actually allowed to say that?

                              BIDEN
I'm sorry. I try to think of myself as a modern kind of
guy, but I simply cannot abide by women using the V-word.

                              WARREN
It's out anatomy, Joe. It's nothing for any of us to be
ashamed of. You sound sexist over there.

                              BIDEN
I cannot be sexist. Some of my best friends are married to
Michelle Obama.

                              Beat.

                              TODD
And with that, I think that we are coming to the end of our
debate this evening. There's just time for our candidates'
closing statements. Senator Bernie Sanders, you can start.

                              SANDERS
Here is my pitch to America. Whatever Elizabeth Warren is
offering to you, you can have it. But at the same time, you
can also satisfy your need to vote for a man because you're
scared of a woman.

                                                    (CONTINUED)

                              MADDOW
Marianne Williamson.

                              WILLIAMSON
Lettuces are the magic fruit. Eat your greens, children.
You can fly darlings.

                              SANDERS
This is why you should never eat anything offered to you by
a stranger.

                              TODD
Beto O'Rourke.

                              O'ROURKE
Nevnte jeg at jeg snakker flytende Spansk?

                              MADDOW
Senator Warren.

                              WARREN
You know, America. I used to be a teacher, so let me all
teach you something now. By definition, a man is only sixty
percent of what a woman is.

                              TODD
Mayor Pete Buttigieg.

                              BUTTIGIEG
Thank you for having me.

                              MADDOW
Senator Harris.

                         HARRIS looks across to make eye
                         contact with BIDEN. As he looks
                         back, she points to her eyes and
                         then at him.

                              TODD
Vice President Biden.

                                              (CONTINUED)

                              BIDEN
America, you've heard many things here tonight. But what I
ask you to do is judge us not on what you hear but on our
actions. When it comes time to decide, judge me on what I
achieved during those eight years I spent in the Biden and
Co. administration. And by Co., I mean Barack Obama.

                              MADDOW
And finally, let's go to Mike Bloomberg.

                         GENERIC WHITE MAN
Well, I --

                    A buzzer interrupts.

                              MADDOW
I'm sorry, but that does mean that we are out of time.

                         GENERIC WHITE MAN
Don't I get to finish?

                              MADDOW
                     (ignoring GENERIC WHITE MAN)
Thank you all for joining us for tonight's debate where --

                              TODD
Where we hope that what you have heard and seen from our
candidates here this evening, will help you make your
decision when it comes time to vote.

                              MADDOW
And for viewers at home disappointed that I cut off Mike
Bloomberg early there, if you'd like to hear more of a
white man talking about issues that others are much more
highly qualified and knowledgeable about, then I invite you
to open your front door and step outside.

                              TODD
Good night.

                              MADDOW
Good night.

                    The light fades.

ACT IV, SCENE TWELVE | MUELLER TESTIFIES

> On stage, the scene is set for a
> CONGRESSIONAL COMMITTEE HEARING
> at the CAPITOL where DEVIN
> NUNES, ADAM SCHIFF, and ERIC
> SWALWELL sit ready to question
> MUELLER who sits in front of
> them.

NARRATOR
(entering)
While the Democrat's search for a new nominee is filled
with action, the President sits hoping that their contest
will provide to him a welcome distraction. For after many
of Trump's closest allies are handed indictment, Robert
Muller is ready to provide the nation with of hope an
incitement --

> The NARRATOR is interrupted by a
> sound similar to flatulence.

SWALWELL
Sorry. I was just moving my chair.

NARRATOR
But as could be predicted, an effort to cover up does soon
ensue, with the Special Counsel's full report permitted to
be read only by a select limited few. And so to uncover the
facts in full, while the White House continues to argue
they're null, in the House a committee date is soon set,
with Democrats hoping to make Republicans sweat. But for
more than one, the goal is not simply the truth to picket,
but instead to gain high-level respect, to gain that
complimentary game ticket.

> The NARRATOR exits.

SCHIFF
Special Counsel Mueller, I'd like to thank you for being
with us today, and if I may, I'd like to begin by going
over the main findings of your report?

(CONTINUED)

                         MUELLER
I would be happy to clarify any point that you need me to.

                         SCHIFF
Thank you. Special Counsel Muller, your report is both
methodical, and it is devastating, for your investigation
determined that the Trump campaign, including Donald Trump
himself, knew that a foreign power was intervening and not
only welcomed it but also used it. Is that correct?

                         MUELLER
                      (nodding)
That is correct.

                         SCHIFF
Your investigation found that the Trump campaign did not
inform the authorities when a foreign power offered dirt on
their opponent. Is that correct?

                         MUELLER
                      (nodding)
That is correct.

                         SCHIFF
You found that instead, they made full use of that offer.
Is that correct?

                         MUELLER
                      (nodding)
That is correct.

                         SCHIFF
Your investigation also found that Donald Trump and his
campaign staff repeatedly lied to investigators, lied to
you, lied to the F-B-I, and lied to this very committee. Is
that correct?

                         MUELLER
                      (nodding)
That is correct.

                                                    (CONTINUED)

                         SCHIFF
Specifically, you found that they lied about meeting and
negotiating with Russian agents, lied about the firing of
James Comey, and lied about wanting to fire you, Director
Mueller. Is that correct?

                         MUELLER
                       (nodding)
That is correct.

                         SCHIFF
Your investigation has already successfully prosecuted
multiple members of Donald Trump's top team, most notably
his former campaign manager, Paul Manafort, and his former
personal lawyer, Michael Cohen. Is that correct?

                         MUELLER
                       (nodding)
That is correct.

                         SCHIFF
Would you personally describe the actions of Donald Trump,
his campaign associates, and the campaign itself, to be a
betrayal of our country?

                         MUELLER
                       (nodding)
I would.

                         SCHIFF
Given your answer just now and taking into account the
findings of your report, do you believe that there are
grounds to indict the President?

                         MUELLER
I cannot answer that.

                         SCHIFF
Director Mueller, speaking on behalf of millions of
Americans, what the hell?

                              Proceedings are interrupted by a
                              sound similar to flatulence.

                                          (CONTINUED)

CONTINUED:

                         SWALWELL
Sorry. I was just moving my glass on the table.

                         MUELLER
Mister Chairman, if I may clarify? I cannot answer that.

                              MUELLER leans forward and makes
                              an obvious wink toward SCHIFF.

                         SCHIFF
I'm sorry, Director Mueller, do you have something stuck in
your eye? We could get you something for that?

                         MUELLER
No. I was just winking to make a point.

                         SCHIFF
That's the end of my questions. Ranking Farmer Nunes.

                         NUNES
Thank you --

                              NUNES turns to SCHIFF.

                         NUNES
You're not funny.

                         SCHIFF
Your concerns have been herd.

                              SCHIFF bangs a gavel.

                         NUNES
                       (to MUELLER)
Director Mueller, on behalf of my Republican colleagues and
myself, I'd like to thank you for your tireless service to
our great nation and for your patriotism, your belief in
and fight for both justice and our rights, and finally, for
conducting yourself always in an honest and honorable way.

                         MUELLER
Thank you for your words.

                                                    (CONTINUED)

NUNES
Now, Director Mueller, could you please explain to us all
why you're a despicable fraud, a liar, a cow --

SWALWELL moos.

NUNES
...ard, and a dishonorable, freedom-hating, partisan
liberal hack that is engaging in this staining of our great
President's record and reputation with all of this, and I'm
going to say it, bull.

SWALWELL moos.

MUELLER
I'm sorry.

NUNES
I asked --

MUELLER
No, I heard you, Mister Nunes. I just did not know that you
knew such big words.

NUNES
Director Mueller, I find your comment deeply offensive. But
the American people find your treasonous witch hunt even
more so. You were tasked with establishing the facts and
instead, you butchered --

SWALWELL moos.

NUNES
...those facts. Not once did you take the time to sit back
and take stock --

SWALWELL moos.

NUNES
...of the full situation. Instead, you steered --

SWALWELL moos.

(CONTINUED)

                             NUNES
...the investigation away from its true purpose of clearing
the President and chose to focus on the Democrats wishes
for you to milk --

                        SWALWELL moos.

                             NUNES
...every small detail for lies that make the President look
bad. And not once throughout this process did you ever even
graze --

                        SWALWELL moos.

                             NUNES
...over the crimes that the Democrats have committed. Well,
let me tell you, Director Mueller, just because the
Democrats have beef --

                        SWALWELL moos.

                             NUNES
...with our President, it doesn't mean that the American
people also do. The truth of it is, anyone who believes any
of the bull --

                        SWALWELL moos.

                           SCHIFF
                        (to SWALWELL)
You've already done that one.

                           SWALWELL
It's still funny.

                             NUNES
                        (to MUELLER)
...in your report must be as thick as leather --

                   SWALWELL and SCHIFF moo.

                             NUNES
Director Mueller, it's time that you were put out to
pasture --

                                              (CONTINUED)

                         SWALWELL begins to moo but cuts
                         himself off.

                    SWALWELL
That one is just too easy.

                         SCHIFF bangs a gavel.

                    SCHIFF
The Ranking Member's time is up. Mr. Swalwell, two minutes.

                    SWALWELL
Thank you, Mister Chairman.
                    (to MUELLER)
Director Mueller, can I just say, it's really great to see
you here today. In fact...

                         SWALWELL stands, a sound similar
                         to flatulence accompanying.

                    SWALWELL
That was my chair again.

                         SWALWELL approaches MUELLER.

                    SWALWELL
This really is a great day for me because it's the day I
get to meet my hero.

                         SWALWELL extends his arm toward
                         MUELLER, and they begin shaking.

                    SWALWELL
But you know, you're not just my hero, Robert. Can I call
you Robert? You are also the hero of many millions of
Americans.

                         In silence, they continue to
                         shake hands.

                         At the side of the stage,
                         unnoticed and filming themselves
                         on a phone, MATT GAETZ and JIM
                         JORDAN enter.

                                             (CONTINUED)

                         MUELLER
I think that we've probably shake long enough now.

                         Beat.

                         SWALWELL
I'm running for President.

                                   SCHIFF bangs a gavel, and
                                   SWALWELL returns to his chair as
                                   the action shifts to GAETZ and
                                   JORDAN.

                         GAETZ
                    (to the phone)
Yo, what is up today, guys? It's me. I'm Matt Gaetz here to
bring you another Gaetz Maetz with my good friend, it's Jim
Jordan, and you can check him our over at Jim Goes Gyming.
We're doing a collab today, isn't that right, Jim?

                         JORDAN
                    (to the phone)
That is right, Matt. We've got something really cool lined
up for all you guys at home.

                         GAETZ
                    (to the phone)
He speaks the truth. Cool is what we do here on Gaetz
Matez, and we do it each and every single day, that's
right, every single day, so you should smack that like
button and subscribe for more content. But onto what we're
showing you guys at home today, it is a big one.

                         JORDAN
                    (to the phone)
Should we tell them what's going on behind us?

                         GAETZ
                    (to the phone)
We should do just that, Jim. Well, guys, behind us is where
the Democrats --

                                                    (CONTINUED)

                    JORDAN
                (to the phone)
Always the Democrats.

                    GAETZ
                (to the phone)
It is always the Democrats. Jim speaks the truth. Behind us
is where the Democrats are hosting a secret interrogation
away from our eyes and, more importantly, away from your
eyes.

                    JORDAN
                (to the phone)
And if you are a patriot who doesn't like what is going on,
then you should leave us a comment in the comment section
below.

                    GAETZ
                (to the phone)
He speaks the truth. Always. But stick around right now
because we are going to crash this party.

                    JORDAN
                (to the phone)
Shall we crash the party?

                    GAETZ
                (to the phone)
Let's crash the party, Jim.

                                GAETZ and JORDAN continue to
                                film themselves as they approach
                                the COMMITTEE.

                    MUELLER
                (mid-conversation)
... Congressman, I do not feel as though that would be an
appropriate thing for me to do.

                    SWALWELL
If you won't endorse me, can we at least get a photo
together?

                                                    (CONTINUED)

                         MUELLER
I can stretch to a ph --

                         GAETZ
                    (to the phone)
Guys, this is what betrayal looks like. This is the
Democrats betraying our country, betraying you, in front of
our very eyes.

              SCHIFF bangs a gavel.

                         SCHIFF
What is going on here?

                         GAETZ
Mister Chairman, I put it to you, in front of the patriots,
our great American patriots who are watching from home our
fight for freedom, that you, Mister Chairman, are a traitor
to our nation.

                         JORDAN
You are holding these secret meetings in private with no
Republicans except for Congressman Nunes, but he doesn't
really count, and you are not letting the American people
watch. What do you have to hide?

                         GAETZ
He speaks the truth. What do you have to hide?

              SCHIFF bangs a gavel.

                         SCHIFF
Congressman Gaetz, Congressman Jordan --

                         GAETZ
You're a disgrace to that chair and to the American people,
Mister chairman.

                         SCHIFF
Congressmen --

                         JORDAN
There should be an investigation into your corruption. I
want hearings. I want indictments --

                                             (CONTINUED)

CONTINUED:

                         MUELLER
Haven't I provided enough of those?

                    SCHIFF bangs a gavel.

                         SCHIFF
Congressmen, this hearing is being broadcast on C-Span.
                    (pointing)
Look. You can see the camcorder over there. A new tape was
put in this morning.

                         GAETZ
You're still denying me and my friend here, both of us
elected representatives, that's right, elected
representatives of our great nation.

                         JORDAN
Are you elected? I didn't think so.

                         GAETZ
He speaks the truth. You are denying us our right to
interrogate...
                    (pointing at MUELLER)
...this traitor.

                         JORDAN
We were going to go all bad cop and bad cop on his ass.

                         MUELLER
Don't you mean good cop, bad cop?

                         JORDAN
No. I was going to be bad cop, and he was going to be worse
cop.

                         GAETZ
He speaks the truth.

                         SCHIFF
Congressmen, the committee on which you both sit heard
testimony from Director Muller just a few hours ago.

                         GAETZ
Don't go changing the subject on us.

                                        (CONTINUED)

                    SCHIFF
I'm calling security.

                         Proceedings are interrupted by a
                         sound similar to flatulence.

                    SWALWELL
Okay. I might need ten minutes this time.

                         SCHIFF bangs a gavel.

                    SCHIFF
Ten minutes.

ACT IV, SCENE THIRTEEN | TRUMP'S MISTAKE

                         The OVAL OFFICE where TRUMP sits
                         at the desk on the phone.

                    NARRATOR
                  (entering)
It is hard to imagine how Mueller could have made his point
clearer, and so it's easy to see how many believe that
impeachment should now be ever nearer. But disappointment
is strong as in the House action is put on hold, for Pelosi
still feels her party's hunt for evidence is coming up
cold. And so feeling in the clear the White House focus now
does shift, as Trump feels the time is right to ensure his
reelection chances do lift. But too far for dirt does the
President push, allowing at last for justice to ambush.

                         The NARRATOR exits.

                    TRUMP
                  (on phone)
It is a lie. They are all lies. A witch hunt. They are
hunting witches, and they think that I am a witch. Fake
news. Robert Mueller is fake news. I did not do anything.
They all hate America. It is so sad.

                         There is a knock on a door, and
                         CONWAY enters.

                                        (CONTINUED)

                         CONWAY
Mister President.

                         TRUMP
                    (on phone)
You wait.
                    (to CONWAY)
Kellyanne Conway, do you want a pizza?

                         CONWAY
Sure, I'll take a Hawaiian.

                         TRUMP
                    (on phone)
And one Hawaiian. And charge the order to Sean Hannity.
Delivered in thirty minutes? Good.

                    TRUMP puts the phone down.

                         TRUMP
I did not think that you liked foreign food?

                         CONWAY
Hawaii isn't foreign, sir.

                         Beat.

                         TRUMP
What can I do for you, Kellyanne Conway?

                         CONWAY
Mister President, I have news about the Democratic Primary.

                         TRUMP
Did you watch the debate? I watched the debate. They were
all losers.

                         CONWAY
Yes, I did watch it, sir.

                         TRUMP
That Bernie Sanders, he looks like the kind of guy who
shouts things at strangers on the A train while everyone
tried to pretend that he is not there.

                                             (CONTINUED)

.

CONTINUED:

                         CONWAY
You've taken the A train before, sir?

                         TRUMP
No. I take the A-plus train because I am super smart.

                         CONWAY
Well, anyway, the latest poll numbers have come out.

                         TRUMP
Am I going to be facing Elizabeth Warren? I have already
been preparing some classic Trump for the debate. I am
going to bring back some old lines. First, I am going to
demand to see her birth certificate, and then I am going to
see her birth certificate, and finally, I am going to
pretend that I never wanted to see her birth certificate.

                         CONWAY
You're not going to be facing Warren, sir. It looks as
though there is a different frontrunner.

                         TRUMP
Who is it?

                         CONWAY
It's Joe Biden, sir.

                         TRUMP
Sleepy Joe Biden? But he is... sleepy.

                         CONWAY
Yes, sir. But he is leading in the polls right now.

                         TRUMP
But I thought that everyone liked Elizabeth Warren and felt
that she did the least worst?

                         CONWAY
Well, yes, that's true, sir. But you're forgetting
something.

                         TRUMP
To book Eric in for his monthly bath?

                                              (CONTINUED)

CONTINUED:

                              CONWAY
I did that for you last night, sir. I meant that Elizabeth
Warren is a woman, and Joe Biden is a man.

                              TRUMP
That is a very good point, Kellyanne Conway.

                              CONWAY
I think this means that we're going to need to change our
approach. We don't have anything on Biden.

                              TRUMP
It is okay, Kellyanne Conway. I know where I can find some
dirt on Joe Biden.

                                        TRUMP stands and approaches an
                                        office window. As he does, a
                                        scene outside the window lights
                                        up where a SMALL BOY wearing a
                                        red shirt is cutting grass.

                              TRUMP
                          (to SMALL BOY)
Do you have any dirt on Joe Biden?

                            SMALL BOY
I don't. I'm sorry, sir.

                              TRUMP
Come here.

                                        The SMALL BOY approaches the
                                        window as TRUMP reaches into his
                                        pocket and pulls out a candy
                                        bar. TRUMP places the candy bar
                                        onto the SMALL BOY's head.

                              TRUMP
Have some candy.

                            SMALL BOY
Thank you, Mister President.

                                                     (CONTINUED)

CONTINUED:

>   The lights on the SMALL BOY go
>   down as TRUMP returns to his
>   desk.

                    TRUMP
He did not have any dirt, Kellyanne Conway.

                    CONWAY
So, what now?

                    TRUMP
I have another idea.

>   TRUMP picks up the phone and
>   dials. A moment later, a pop
>   song begins to play as a
>   spotlight finds PUTIN at the
>   other side of the stage.
>
>   PUTIN pulls out his phone and
>   answers, and the song stops as
>   he does.

                    PUTIN
                  (on phone)
Donald. How be you?

                    TRUMP
                  (on phone)
Vladimir Putin, I have news.

                    PUTIN
                  (on phone)
Do tell Putin what it be.

                    TRUMP
                  (on phone)
Elizabeth Warren and Joe Biden are both sad losers, but Joe
Biden is slightly less sad and slightly less of a loser.

                    PUTIN
                  (on phone)
You mean United States voters not prefer highly qualified
woman with real ideas over man who sometime act creepy?

                                           (CONTINUED)

CONTINUED:

                    TRUMP
                 (on phone)
Yes.

                    PUTIN
                 (on phone)
I know that already. Putin know that for four years.

                    TRUMP
                 (on phone)
What are we going to do?

                    PUTIN
                 (on phone)
I have plan.

                    TRUMP
                 (on phone)
A good plan?

                    PUTIN
                 (on phone)
All plan be good of mine. In Russia I be known as Putin the
plan planner. I call back later.

                         TRUMP puts the phone down as
                         PUTIN exits.

                    TRUMP
                 (to CONWAY)
We have a plan.

                         The lights on the OVAL OFFICE
                         fade as lights go up on the
                         scene at a SUPERMARKET CASH
                         REGISTER, where OBAMA stands in
                         line behind a CUSTOMER being
                         served by the CASHIER.

                    CASHIER
That will be eleven dollars four cents.

                                              (CONTINUED)

                              BIDEN enters with his own
                              shopping and stands in line
                              behind OBAMA.

                              As the CUSTOMER pays, BIDEN
                              unsuccessfully attempts to get
                              OBAMA's attention.

                    CASHIER
Thank you for shopping with us.
                    (to OBAMA)
Next, please.

                              As the CUSTOMER exits, OBAMA
                              moves forward and places his
                              basket on the counter.

                    OBAMA
Just this small selection... of your most excellent items
of fresh, ripe produce, commodious goods... and tradable
essential daily commodities today please, good sir.

                              BIDEN attempts to get his
                              attention once more.

                    OBAMA
                 (turning to BIDEN)
Joe, I know that you're standing in that space... What are
you doing here?

                    BIDEN
Barack. I never saw you there. What are you doing here?

                    OBAMA
I'm here to tender authentic United States currency for a
variety of items... which my family and I require... What
are you doing here?

                    BIDEN
What a coincidence. I'm here doing my shopping too. We're
so alike, aren't we?

                                              (CONTINUED)

CONTINUED:

OBAMA
But, Joe, this establishment is a considerable distance
from... the locality in which you and your wife cohabit...
Like many hundreds of miles away.

BIDEN
Well, you know, I often think that this place has...

> BIDEN looks around and grabs an
> onion from a nearby stand.

BIDEN
The best gosh damn potatoes in America.

CASHIER
(to BIDEN)
Sir, that's an onion, and I told you yesterday, please
don't keep touching our produce. If you start sniffing the
fruit again, then I'll have to call my supervisor.

OBAMA
You transported yourself hundreds of miles to get yourself
a real good potato... that is actually an onion?

BIDEN
What can I say? I like fresh food.

OBAMA
Joe, have you been frequenting this branch... of a well-
known grocery store chain in the hope... that you might run
into me?

BIDEN
No, of course not. Though while I'm seeing you, how is
Michelle and the girls? Oh, and have you decided on that
endorsement yet?

OBAMA
I've already communicated my position on this matter... I'm
not making any decision... on who yet to endow with my
words of recommendation.

(CONTINUED)

                         BIDEN
Come on, Barack. I could really do with a hand, and I've
always had your back.

                         OBAMA
It wouldn't be correct or just of me to cause... any
splitting of factions, beliefs, or other ideals within...
the Democratic Party at this time.

                         CASHIER
                       (to OBAMA)
That comes to seventeen dollars and twenty-nine cents,
Mister President.

                    OBAMA hands over a bill.

                         OBAMA
Here is a twenty-dollar bill... Keep the change.

                         CASHIER
Thank you, Mister President.

                         BIDEN
                       (to OBAMA)
Well, how about we just get a photo together?

                         OBAMA
I don't currently have the availability in the schedule of
my day... to fulfill the request that you make of me...
Perhaps some other time.

                    OBAMA exits and leaves BIDEN
                    looking after him.

                         BIDEN
                       (to CASHIER)
What about you? Will you endorse me?

                    PUTIN enters dressed as another
                    cashier.

                         PUTIN
                       (to CASHIER)
You be needed at customer servicing desk.

                                        (CONTINUED)

                         CASHIER
What's happened?

                         PUTIN
There be woman called Karen there who claims she had only
ninety-nine sheets of toilet paper on roll she bought
instead of advertised one hundred. She wants to speak to
manager.

                         CASHIER
Oh, boy. I best go sort it out.

                         PUTIN
Good. I take over here.

                              The CASHIER exits as PUTIN takes
                              their place.

                         PUTIN
                       (to BIDEN)
Hello, and welcome to big shop. How can I help today?

                              BIDEN places his basket on the
                              counter.

                         BIDEN
What about you? You'll endorse me, right?

                         PUTIN
I endorse you? Sure. I endorse you.

                         BIDEN
Well, that's someone, at least.

                         PUTIN
You seem like there be stuff that bother you. Why not tell
me what it be? Perhaps you feel better after.

                         BIDEN
I'm not sure about that. I don't normally talk about this
stuff.

                         PUTIN
You trust me. I be your... greengrocer.

                                              (CONTINUED)

                         BIDEN
I'm not so sure.

                              PUTIN pulls a candy bar and
                              vegetable from the basket.

                         PUTIN
                    (holding up the candy)
Eat less of this.
                    (holding up the vegetable)
Eat more of this. Also, cat milk. It not come from real
cat.

                         BIDEN
I don't understand?

                         PUTIN
Now I also be doctor you can trust.

                         BIDEN
Well, alright. Recently it has just felt like even though
I'm still popular, people just don't seem to like me
anymore.

                         PUTIN
I see.

                              PUTIN takes a melon from the
                              basket.

                         BIDEN
And then there's my son, Hunter Biden. He's been having a
stressful time in his job in Ukraine.

                              PUTIN drops the melon onto his
                              foot.

                         BIDEN
And then there are the annoying neighbors next door.

                         PUTIN
What was that?

                                             (CONTINUED)

                        BIDEN
The neighbors? A couple called Makayla and Josh.

                        PUTIN
No. Before that.

                        BIDEN
My son, Hunter Biden?

                        PUTIN
Tell me more.

                        BIDEN
Well, he does some work out in Ukraine. It's a nice job
he's got there too. Stressful at times, though.

                        PUTIN
                     (to himself)
I be sure I find way to use that.

                        BIDEN
I'm sorry?

                        PUTIN
I said shopping be twenty-three dollar.

                        BIDEN
Of course.

                                  BIDEN reaches into his pocket
                                  and pulls out a handful of
                                  quarters.

                        BIDEN
                 (to himself, counting)
One quarter. Two quarters. Three quarters. One Dollar.

                        PUTIN
Actually, today for you, special offer. It be free.

                        BIDEN
Are you sure?

                                      (CONTINUED)

CONTINUED:

> PUTIN
> It not make difference to me. I not own store.

> BIDEN
> Well, thank you very much, young man.

> PUTIN
> Now go. I have phone call to make.

> BIDEN
> See you around.

>> BIDEN exits with his shopping as
>> PUTIN pulls out his phone and
>> dials.
>>
>> At the other side of the stage,
>> a phone rings out, and the
>> lights go back up on TRUMP sat
>> in the OVAL OFFICE.

> TRUMP
> (on phone)
> You are through to Donald J. Trump. Calls to this number
> cost thirteen Dollars a minute. Now tell me what are you
> wearing?

> PUTIN
> (on phone)
> About half a broken watermelon on left shoe.

> TRUMP
> (on phone)
> Comrade Vladimir Putin, I did not realize it was you.

> PUTIN
> (on phone)
> Donald, listen carefully. I have dirt on Joe Biden. He have
> son who do business in Ukraine.

> TRUMP
> (on phone)
> What is a Ukraine?

(CONTINUED)

                         PUTIN
                    (on phone)
It be part of Europe that Russia not own yet. Like Russia's
Canada.

                         TRUMP
                    (on phone)
So what do I need to do?

                         PUTIN
                    (on phone)
Dig deep. Get more dirt. Find more information and use it
against Joe Biden. Crush opponent.

                              The CASHIER returns to PUTIN's
                              side.

                    CASHIER
Excuse me, sir.

                         PUTIN
                    (on phone)
Donald, I must go. I be needed.

                              PUTIN and TRUMP both put their
                              phones down.

                    CASHIER
Sir, I forgot to check. Do you actually work here?

                              PUTIN picks up a broken half of
                              melon from the floor and hands
                              it to the CASHIER.

                         PUTIN
Here. Have present.

                              PUTIN and the CASHIER exits as
                              the lights on the SUPERMARKET
                              CASH REGISTER scene go down, and
                              action returns to the OVAL
                              OFFICE.

                                             (CONTINUED)

CONTINUED:

                         TRUMP
                    (to himself)
Okay. I need to make this big. What do I do? I know. I
should be super smart and blackmail Ukraine.

                              TRUMP picks up his phone and
                              dials.

                              As a phone rings out, a light
                              finds OBAMA who pulls his phone
                              from his pocket and answers.

                         OBAMA
                    (on phone)
Now really, Joe, this situation is beginning to develop...
into an out of hand set of circumstances... I don't yet
know who I'm endorsing --

                         TRUMP hangs up.

                         OBAMA
                    (to himself)
He hung up on me.
                    (exiting)
Hey, Michelle. Joe hung up on me.

                              As the light goes down on OBAMA,
                              TRUMP dials again.

                         TRUMP
I will try this number.

                              As another phone rings out, a
                              light finds ERIC.

                         ERIC
                    (on phone)
Hello. You're through to Eric. My name is Eric. What's your
name?

                         TRUMP
                    (on phone)
Eric --

                                                  (CONTINUED)

                    ERIC
                 (on phone)
     Hey, that's cool. I'm called Eric too.

                    TRUMP
                 (on phone)
     Eric Trump, get off the phone. I am trying to call Ukraine.

                         TRUMP hangs up as the light on
                         ERIC goes down.

                    TRUMP
     How can it be so hard to call a country?

                         TRUMP dials again as a light
                         finds WILLIAMSON.

                    WILLIAMSON
                 (on phone)
     Are you calling to share the love?

                         TRUMP hangs up quickly, and the
                         light goes down.

                    TRUMP
     Okay. It has to be this one.

                         TRUMP dials once more as this
                         time, a light finds TIFFANY
                         TRUMP.

                    TRUMP
                 (on phone)
     Hello. This is Donald J. Trump.

                    TIFFANY
                 (on phone)
     Father?

                    TRUMP
                 (on phone)
     Who is this?

                                             (CONTINUED)

                    TIFFANY
                 (on phone)
I'm your daughter.

                    TRUMP
                 (on phone)
Ivanka?

                    TIFFANY
                 (on phone)
Tiffany.

                    TRUMP
                 (on phone)
I do not have any money.

                         TRUMP hangs up as the light goes
                         down.

                    TRUMP
This is the last number that I have.

                         TRUMP dials a final time, and a
                         phone begins to ring out. A
                         pause follows before,
                         eventually, a voice answers.

                    PELOSI (IN DARKNESS)
                 (on phone)
Hello.

                    TRUMP
                 (on phone)
Now listen here. I want dirt on sleepy Joe Biden. I want to
know everything that you have got. What is he doing in
Ukraine? Why is he in Ukraine? Make it up if you have to.
Tell me everything or America will make it not so good to
be Ukraine.

                    PELOSI (IN DARKNESS)
                 (on phone)
Who is this?

                                        (CONTINUED)

CONTINUED:

> TRUMP
> (on phone)

Do not play dumb with me. I am President Donald J. Trump of the United States of America.

> PELOSI (IN DARKNESS)
> (on phone)

President Trump?

>> A spotlight shines on a table
>> where PELOSI and SCHUMER sit
>> drinking coffee.

> PELOSI
> (to SCHUMER)

It's the President.

> TRUMP
> (on phone)

Some people say the best ever President Trump.

> PELOSI
> (on phone)

This is Nancy Pelosi.
> (beat, then to SCHUMER)

Chuck, I think that we've got him.

> Beat.

> SCHUMER

Oh, good. I'll go and change my facial expression to something more appropriate.

> SCHUMER exits.

> PELOSI
> (on phone)

Donald? Are you there, Donald?

>> Slowly, TRUMP puts his phone
>> down and stares straight ahead.

>> (CONTINUED)

PELOSI
(on phone)
Donald?

TRUMP
Oh no.

> Lights out.

ACT IV, SCENE FOURTEEN | TRUMP'S FINAL EXIT

> The NARRATOR enters a spotlight at the side of an otherwise dark and empty stage.

NARRATOR
And so at least it seems perhaps that the President's time in office is soon set to lapse. For asking for dirt from a foreign nation can be considered by none to be an innocent vocation. The accurate account of what happened next is one that all sat here are sure to know. No justice, no truth, no hope, and not something we wish to show. And so instead, we present to you our interpretation of what we feel should have been, Donald J. Trump's final exit scene.

> The NARRATOR exits as another lights go up on PELOSI and SCHUMER (smiling broadly) stood at a podium to address the audience.

PELOSI
Good morning.

SCHUMER
My colleague is right. It is a good morning, and that is why I am smiling at you all today.

PELOSI
We are pleased to have this opportunity to tell you all about a bad thing that the President did last night. But it did not involve a checkbook.

(CONTINUED)

                          SCHUMER
That is right. Instead, the President called Nancy here --

                          PELOSI
                       (to SCHUMER)
Am I telling the story, or are you telling the story?

                          SCHUMER
Please accept my apology for interrupting you.

                          PELOSI
That is quite okay.

                          SCHUMER
And may I thank you for holding me to account.

                          PELOSI
                       (to audience)
Last night, at approximately seventeen minutes past eight,
the President called me while I was having drinks with
Chuck here. These drinks, of course, were of a strictly
professional nature.

                          SCHUMER
What Nancy means is that we did not go on to do the dancing
of the Paphian jig together.

                          PELOSI
Chuck is correct. At no point was congress amorous. We did
not, as the young people say, do the blanket hornpipe, ride
below the crupper, or even make butter with one's tail.

                          Beat.

                          PELOSI
The nature of the President's call was to ask Ukraine for
incriminating information on Joe Biden.

                          SCHUMER
Which is a bad thing to do.

                          PELOSI
It is a bad thing to do, and that is why earlier this
morning, I informed the authorities of this phone call.

                                                    (CONTINUED)

SCHUMER
Which is a good thing to do.

PELOSI
It is a good thing to do, and I am pleased that they have
already issued warrants for the arrests of President Donald
Trump, and his son's, Donald Trump Junior, and Eric Trump.

SCHUMER
Which is going to be beautiful to watch.

PELOSI
It is going to be beautiful to watch. We hope you enjoy it.

                           PELOSI and SCHUMER exit as
                           silence and darkness falls.

JUNIOR (IN DARKNESS)
So, you know, I think that this way is the way out.

TRUMP (IN DARKNESS)
Why can we not just run away to South America again?

JUNIOR (IN DARKNESS)
We can't get there. Don't you remember? Last week you
pulled out a map and banned flights to and from everywhere
that you thought was China.

TRUMP (IN DARKNESS)
Some people say that it was a smart move.

JUNIOR (IN DARKNESS)
But it means that we can't escape. And this map you've
given me doesn't help.

TRUMP (IN DARKNESS)
What is wrong with it?

JUNIOR (IN DARKNESS)
Eric cut it off the back of a cereal box.

ERIC (IN DARKNESS)
I got to use grown-up scissors.

                                            (CONTINUED)

                         JUNIOR (IN DARKNESS)
According to this, the talking cartoon alligator should be
on our left.

                         TRUMP (IN DARKNESS)
I cannot see anything.

                         JUNIOR (IN DARKNESS)
It's too dark.

                         TRUMP (IN DARKNESS)
I have an idea. I am going to bleach my eyes to see better.

                    Beat.

                         JUNIOR (IN DARKNESS)
Does that work?

                         From the darkness comes a slight
                         dripping sound.

                         TRUMP (IN DARKNESS)
No. Everything has gone funny.

                         A thud follows as TRUMP trips
                         and hits the floor.

                         TRUMP (IN DARKNESS)
Eric Trump, what are you doing down here?

                         The scene becomes dimly lit as
                         JUNIOR lights a torch.

                         ERIC
I found a nickel on the floor.

                         TRUMP
That nickel is mine. I dropped it earlier.

                         JUNIOR
Can we talk about this later? We need to get out of here
before --

                                              (CONTINUED)

>   As ERIC and TRUMP both stand, a
>   large, bright searchlight
>   appears on them.

                         JUNIOR
...anyone notices us.

>   A beat, and then Russian banjo
>   music accompanies their
>   suspicious movements to one
>   side. As they stop, the music
>   stops.
>
>   Another beat, and then the same
>   music as they move the other
>   way. Again, it stops as they
>   stop.

                         JUNIOR
Okay, so, you know, I think we're going to have to run.

>   A third beat, and then the music
>   continues as ERIC, JUNIOR, and
>   TRUMP run offstage.
>
>   A moment later, two FBI AGENTS
>   enter from the other side of the
>   stage and give chase.
>
>   As the two FBI AGENTS exits,
>   ERIC, JUNIOR, and TRUMP reenter
>   and stop in the middle of the
>   stage.

                         TRUMP
                       (to JUNIOR)
We need to ditch the stupid one.

                         JUNIOR
                       (to ERIC)
Okay, buddy. We're going to play a game of hide and seek.
You count first.

                                              (CONTINUED)

                          ERIC
Okay. Let's have fun. One... seven... four... nine...

                              As ERIC stands counting with his
                              hands covering his face, JUNIOR
                              and TRUMP make their exit.

                              The FBI AGENTS return and walk
                              up to ERIC. After a moment, they
                              grab him and begin to drag him
                              toward the wings.

                          ERIC
                        (exiting)
...five... eight... eleven... Hey, is this an earthquake?

                              With the stage one more empty, a
                              brick wall is brought on from
                              the wings to meet JUNIOR and
                              TRUMP reentering from the other
                              side of the stage.

                              Noticing the wall, JUNIOR
                              doubles back to the wings to
                              bring out a ladder.
                              JUNIOR begins to scale the wall,
                              as he reaches the top, however,
                              TRUMP takes a run-up and hits
                              the wall with enough force to
                              knock it, and JUNIOR, over.

                              TRUMP makes his exit as the two
                              FBI AGENTS return to retrieve
                              and unconscious JUNIOR.

                              This time, TRUMP enters the
                              stage walking backward as the
                              two FBI AGENTS do the same from
                              the other side.

                                                    (CONTINUED)

>   Stopping close to each other,
>   simultaneously, they all look
>   behind each other in such a way
>   as to not notice anyone else.
>
>   As a group, they turn clockwise
>   and then back again.
>
>   Finally, at the same time, they
>   all turn around and notice each
>   other.
>
>   A beat, and then TRUMP turns,
>   takes two sarcastic steps
>   forward and then makes a run for
>   it. As he reaches the wings,
>   however, he is tackled suddenly
>   to the ground by CLINTON.
>
>   As the FBI AGENTS close in on
>   TRUMP, CLINTON stands, brushes
>   her hands together, and turns to
>   address the audience.

                              CLINTON
You have no idea how satisfying that was.

ACT IV, SCENE FIFTEEN | CLINTON IN THE OVAL OFFICE

>   The NARRATOR enters an otherwise
>   empty OVAL OFFICE.

                              NARRATOR
And so, at last, we reach the end, though certainly truth
we will now bend. For no matter how much we hope, wish, or
to you portray, at least now, accountability will not take
place on any nearby day. Our story was one neither all
accurate or whole, and as you leave, democracy still misses
its long lost soul. But while laughter was why you all
gathered in this here place, we ask that you exit with just
one message we hope you will ensure to pass along. A
message that can only be delivered by the woman who, from
the start, remained strong.

                                            (CONTINUED)

                              The NARRATOR exits as CLINTON
                              enters.

                         CLINTON
                       (to audience)
Be honest, you missed me, didn't you? Now, America. I do
not want to say that I told you so, but I did tell you so.

I told you all that Donald Trump would be a bad president.
I told you that he was not qualified. I told you that he
would ruin our standing in the world. I told you that he
would try to start wars with countries that he can't spell.
I told you that he would destroy our economy. And I told
you that he would try to kill us all. I guess what I am
trying to say, America, is that I was right.

Do you all remember that time you thought that a woman is
too emotional to be president? Or when you all said that I
was not likable enough. Well, let me ask you this, America.
How do you like me now?

I am not here to gloat, however. There will be an eternity
for that when we are all in hell together. Or Tampa as they
call it in some parts. I am here to give you all one final
reminder. Not about switching off your devices, but about
all of us here in this room.

We have faced difficult times under President Trump. And
many of us will indeed continue to do so because the
reality is, some people are very stupid. But this fact does
not mean that any of us should ever give up, or that we
should shut up. And you can trust me, I know about not
shutting up.

Now if you take just one thing from this here show tonight,
other than memories of the uncomfortable seats, overpriced
soda, and the strange smell coming from the end cubicle in
the bathroom, then let it be a reminder of the knowledge
that every person in this room has the power to make a
difference. Well, almost everyone. I am not so sure about
the person sat in seat E-eleven. After all, they are
responsible for that end cubicle.

                         (MORE)
                                               (CONTINUED)

CONTINUED:

                        CLINTON (CONT'D)
But we all, in our own way, contribute to the world and the
lives of those we know and meet. And we all have the power
to stand up for what we believe in and for a future where
everyone is both equal and safe, and where our planet is
protected for people to enjoy that future.

If we all make an effort to show a little kindness and
respect, and we work to inspire and lift others, then
maybe, we can be strong enough to make it through anything.

                        CLINTON approaches the desk.

                        CLINTON
But now, it is time for the moment that you have all been
waiting for.

                        CLINTON sniffs and gently
                        strokes the desk.

                        CLINTON
It is mine. All mine. I have waited centuries for this.

                        CLINTON goes to sit in the
                        chair.

                        CLINTON
Shall I do it? I am going to do it. I am doing it.

                        CLINTON sits in the chair and
                        holds out her hands.

                        CLINTON
Ha. Ha. Ha. Finally. I AM YOUR PRESIDENT --

                        CLINTON is cut off as the desk
                        swivels around to revel PENCE
                        sat at the other side.

                        CONWAY
                      (entering)
President Pence, sir.

                        Filled with rage, CLINTON walks
                        back into view.

                                            (CONTINUED)

                         CLINTON
NO!

                    Lights out.

               THE END

CPSIA information can be obtained
at www.ICGtesting.com
Printed in the USA
BVHW071624111120
593051BV00015B/639